She Fell in love with A

Dope Boy 3

Miss Candice

© **2017**
Published by Leo Sullivan Presents

Previously

"Where were you?" I asked, as I lied there wrapped in his strong arms.

"Handlin' business," he said as he massaged my scalp.

"I missed you... You couldn't text...call... nothing?"

"Nah baby. I wanted to bad as fuck but—"

"But why couldn't you just take me with you. You was fuckin off with a bitch or something?"

He honestly told me, "I was torturing a nigga for three days."

"Wait... what?"

"You talkin out cha ass so I kept it a band with you."

"You still could have text or something."

He did not understand what I went through. He didn't know how petrified I was. Being without him affected me in ways I never wanted to be affected in again. I didn't like it. I hated it.

"I didn't have my phone. Besides, you was aight. I'm sure you were occupied with the nigga you were supposed to leave well before I disappeared," he coldly said.

"I'm trying to," I said as I rolled my eyes to the back of my head.

"If you were trying, you wouldn't have pulled away when I was sucking on your neck a minute ago, sweetheart."

Should I tell him? I hadn't told Cass anything about the way Dinero had been acting. He didn't know Dinero threatened to kill himself if I left him. His crazy ass would probably offer to kill the nigga himself. I didn't tell him that I was worried about what Shonny said. I didn't tell him that the fear I had of leaving him was no longer based on Cassim's lifestyle alone. I was dead ass worried about some homicide, suicide shit popping off.

"Give me a little—"

"I'm not giving you anymore time. I told you... time was of the essence and I wasn't about to sit back being a whole ass side nigga, baby," said Cass shutting me up.

I had to leave him. I didn't have any other choice but to.

*

A week had passed since Cass came back and he was still on me about leaving Dinero. Thing is, I'd been trying to. But things had been crazy down at the hospital with Peewee and he was barely ever around. I felt like I owed him more than to break up with him through text message. That might have been the best thing to do since he was always too irrational when it came to me trying to leave his crazy ass.

After not seeing and barely talking to him for a week, he pops up ironically while I'm sitting on the couch reading directions for a pregnancy test. My period was a few days late and I was hella noid. That bitch showed up like clockwork every month. My shit was so dead on that I even came on at the same time of day. So when she didn't show up, I was worried.

I quickly tossed the unopened box behind me, but I wasn't fast enough and he'd seen it. His eyebrows knitted together, and he quickly snatched it from behind me.

"You pregnant?" he asked with worry written all over his face.

I snatched it from his hands, "I obviously don't know yet."

Dinero ran his hand over his wave covered head and said, "Go take it."

"How is Peewee? Are things looking up," I asked, trying to avoid taking the test in front of him.

"Yeah, his vitals are returning to normal and he's been eating," he quickly replied before telling me to go take the test again.

I sighed and pushed myself up from the couch, heading down to the bathroom. He tried to walk inside with me, but I put my hand up, blocking him.

"Wait," I said before closing the door in his face.

I pulled my shorts down and sat on the toilet staring at the stick, scared to take it. I still didn't know what went on between Dinero and I when I was drunk. He said he wasn't sure if he used a condom or not, and by the dry cum sitting on my thigh that day, I was sure that he didn't. And I knew for a fact that Cass came inside of me because I let him.

I leaned forward and pissed on the stick, then sat it on the counter. My leg bounced with anticipation as I thought about just how much a positive test would change everything. I would have to tell Cass that I was pregnant and that I didn't know who the baby would belong to. I would have to break his heart. I wasn't supposed to have sex with Dinero anymore. My pussy belonged to Cass. I told him that. Now I would have to tell him that I'd given it to Dinero. But...I was drunk... he would understand that, right? Shit no he wouldn't. Cass was a ticking time bomb and he's already been waiting long enough for me to officially be his. He would most likely be tired of my shit and just be done with me.

Knock. Knock. Knock.

"Ay baby, let me come in," said Dinero from the other side of the door.

I didn't want him in here with me. I wanted to experience this alone. My anxiety was already to the roof. My foot tapped against the white tile of the bathroom floor as I nervously chewed on my freshly manicured nails, staring at the test sitting on the sink.

I looked down at my Michael Kors watch. It was time to check the results.

"Ryann—

"Hold on, okay?"

"What does it say? Am I a daddy or what? This shit is fucked up. I should be—

"Shut up," I yelled. I sighed, "Please... just let me do this alone."

He fell silent and I picked the pregnancy test up. Staring at the two pink lines, a knot immediately grew in my throat.

"Ryann... am I a daddy?"

I looked down at the positive pregnancy test, speechless.

I didn't know. Not knowing fucked me up. Not knowing petrified me.

Life had a fucked up sense of humor. And I didn't find anything about this shit to be funny.

"Ryann—

"Dinero... go home! I'll call you," I yelled with a trembling voice, trying to figure out what I was going to do about this positive pregnancy test.

He banged on the door, "What the fuck do you mean go home?"

My eyebrows snapped together as I began to have a flashback about the last night I had sex with Dinero. The tone of his voice when he asked me what I meant just go home was familiar.... It was of the same tone he used when I tried to push him off of me that night, when I told him to get the fuck out of my house and go home.

But he didn't leave. He pinned me down and forced my panties down.

"Dinero.... Did you rape me?"

Silence.

"Did you hear what the fuck I just asked you, nigga?" I yelled as I jumped up from the toilet.

"I'm sorry," he said before I heard the front door open.

I quickly snatched the bathroom door open and ran out of the bathroom trying to beat him before he left, but he was already gone. I pulled my shorts up and ran for the front door, but he was already speeding from in front of the house. Tears fell from eyes as I closed the door and snatched my phone from the coffee table. I called Goose and he answered almost immediately.

"What's good, Ry baby?"

"Dinero raped me," I said through clenched teeth as I sealed Dinero's fate.

Chapter One . Cass

I woke up to the sound of my ringing doorbell.

Ding. Dong.

Reaching over to the nightstand where the small remote control sat, I brought life to the TV screen hanging from the ceiling a few feet away from my bed.

Jane. Mothafuckin Jane.

She smiled brightly and waved at the camera while holding a cherry pie up, "I've brought pie—

"I don't want none of ya flavorless ass pie, Jane. Go home."

She frowned and placed a piece of hair behind her ear before stepping closer to the camera, "After I suck the cherry filling off that huge cock of yours."

I rubbed sleep from my eyes and sighed, "Go home to your husband, Jane. Fucked up my homie done got caught up with such a whore for a wife."

"I wasn't a whore when you shoved your penis down my throat," she barked.

I laughed, "Actually, darlin... you were."

She raised the pie she had in her hands and started to throw it on my door. But the booming sound of my voice blaring through the speaker, daring her to do it, stopped her before she could. She shook hair out of her face, turned on her heels and walked away.

My phone started to ring and I leaned over to grab it from the nightstand

"What's good, fam," I said as I answered my ringing phone.

"Redrum," said Juice through gritted teeth.

"You on the block," I asked as I jumped up from the bed.

"Yeah, bro. Get here," said Juice before hanging up.

As soon as we hung up, I slipped my Nike slides on and headed out the front door.

*

I pulled up on the block thirty minutes later. I jumped straight up and headed to the block, didn't shower, shit, or brush my teeth. A nigga yell redrum, some shit is definitely up. And since Juice was calling me, with two looney tune ass brothers on his team, told me that the murder mission he was on pertained to Ryann.

For Ryann, I would go to war with a whole fuckin' country.

I hopped out the whip and mobbed up to the house. The first thing I noticed was Ryann's whip missing. I'd called and text her and she ain't replied to none of them shits. I was hot and on tip. Anybody was liable to catch a slug or two at this point.

Juice and Adrien came out of the house and immediately slapped hands with me before we went into the house.

Juice took a long pull from his blunt before passing it to me.

Adrien paced the floor back and forth, loading a burner.

"What's poppin?" I asked before pulling from the blunt. "Whose heart do I need to cut out of their chest?"

Dead ass.

I would dead ass hop on some surgical shit over my Ryann.

"Dinero violated on a level no nigga on earth should ever violate on," said Juice with tight lips.

My eyebrows shot up and my top lip turned up in a frown, "Fuck you talm'bout nigga? Elaborate. Let me hear it."

"He raped her," said Adrien with his eyes up, but his head slightly turned down. "He straight took pussy from sis."

"Yo, what," I yelled.

Rape? He raped my shorty. I've always took Dinero for a bitch-nigga. But this shit here? Nah, I never expected this.

A few seconds later, the storm door swung open, and five more niggas stepped into the crib. Out of the five, I recognized all of them. I slapped hands with Loc and he then did the same with Juice and Adrien. When the other four niggas came at me to slap hands, I turned away from them. I'm not a friendly nigga. I don't give a fuck if I did see 'em around the way. Them niggas weren't my niggas.

I pushed through the crowd and headed for the front door.

"Yo, where you goin, Cass?" yelled Loc.

"Fuck you think I'm going?" I shot back over my shoulder. "You niggas standing around, talkin', but nah...I'm going to do work."

"Standing around? Nigga you off ya shit if you think that's what's going on right now," yelled Juice. "We don't stand around, boss. We do work. Fuck you talm'bout? We been beating blocks heavy all fuckin' night trying to find that pussy nigga. He disappeared. Up and vanished like a ghost. This right here? Nigga we posted, trying to strategize. All fuckin' night and morning... for hours... trying to find him. You sound bout goofy as fuck if you—"

I chuckled and ran my tongue over my bottom lip, "You slick talkin', Juice." I pointed. "Watch your mouth, G."

"Aight, aight, aight," said Loc before sitting down on the couch. "Be cool. We're all here for the same reason. Ryann. Fuck we gone accomplish if we got animosity towards each other? Nothing."

"Fuck we gone accomplish sitting in a house full of niggas? Nothing," I said before pushing the storm door open.

I ran down the steps as I fished around my pocket from my phone. My left eye twitched as I listened to her phone go to voicemail for the fourth time.

"Hey Cass—"

"Fuck is Ryann?" I asked her cousin, interrupting her.

She sucked her teeth, "I don't know nigga. And if you really mad because Ryann said Dinero raped her, you wastin ya time. That nigga did not rape her. She bent over and took that dick. Bitch lying, looking for attention."

I ran my tongue over the corner of my mouth and said, "Yo, you might wanna watch what flies out of that slut ass mouth of yours, aight?"

"LeeLee," yelled one of the niggas who walked into the crib with Loc.

LeeLee rolled her eyes and sucked her teeth, "Nigga—

"Ashlee," yelled another one of them.

"What Henny? What Boo," she yelled back, marching up the stairs to them. "Damn!"

"Stop running yo fuckin' mouth so much," said one of them.

I hopped in the whip, cranked the engine up, and scurred off from in front of the house. Bird ass bitch just didn't know how close she was to getting the piss smacked out of her. She was popping off recklessly because she wanted the dick. Bitch been tripping ever since I offered to fuck, and didn't. Since she was bitter, she wanted me to think my shorty was a liar. But I know Ryann, and if baby said she got raped... she got raped.

I punched the steering wheel before gripping it with trembling hands. I was enraged and needed to know why the fuck Ry was ignoring me. I had just talked to baby the night before. I knew something was up about her mood. She kept saying she was tired, so I let her go.

I slammed down on the brakes at the sight of Dinero's sister posted up on the porch. I shifted the car in park and hopped out. As soon as she peeped me coming up the stairs, she rolled her eyes and sighed.

"I don't know where Dinero—

I wrapped my hands around her neck and backed her up against the house. I didn't give a fuck that that bitch was flooded with hoodrats from around the way. I didn't give a fuck about the old heads across the street watching me either.

"Let her go, Cass," yelled Tiny, grabbing my bicep.

I flung her off my arm and she fell into the chairs.

"Oh my God, Tiny, are you okay?" yelled one of the other girls. "She's pregnant, nigga!"

I mugged at her, "Fuck I look like? Am I supposed to care?"

"Shonny—Shonny don't know where Dinero is. I swear to God," said Tiny, picking herself up from the porch.

Shonny clawed at my hand with tears streaming down her face. I let her go and walked away. I snatched the storm door to the crib open and walked straight inside. Her peoples were sitting on the couch, laughing at The Real.

They didn't even know a whole ass stranger had walked into their crib. They sat on the couch laughing their asses off. It wasn't until the mother turned around to say something to who she thought was Shonny, that she jumped up.

"James," she yelled to her husband.

James turned around to see what had his wife so shook and jumped up from the couch when he got a look at me.

"Where ya son at," I casually asked as I walked further into the living room.

"Shondra honey, who is this man?" asked the mother after Shonny walked into the house.

"Get out of my house. Dinero don't live here," said the father standing in front of his wife.

I continued into living room until I was standing right at the coffee table. I reached over and grabbed a handful of the wrapped mints sitting in a dish. I stuffed all but one in my pocket.

"I didn't ask if he lived here," I said as I unwrapped the mint. "I asked you where he was."

"Sandra, go into the room—"

"Nah, Sandra, stay right where you are, darlin," I said, interrupting him as I popped the mint into my mouth. She tried to inch from behind him and I pulled my banger from my waistband, "I think you should stay where you are, Sandra. Unless you want me to paint these white walls red."

"Cass... listen," said Shonny, creeping away from the door with her hands up. "We really don't know where Dinero is. He called, said he loved us, and left."

"Why should I believe you," I asked. "Convince me."

Shonny's eyebrows snapped together and from the corner of my eye I could see James making slight movements. I cocked the hammer to the burner back and aimed it at Sandra's head.

"You must like red, James," I said as I moved the mint around in my mouth.

"How...how can I convince you?" asked Shonny.

I rubbed my chin with my freehand and said, "Who do you love more? Your brother, or your mother?"

I pressed the barrel of the burner against Sandra's head and James lost it. At least he attempted to. As soon as he moved, I took the gun from Sandra's forehead and let one off near James' foot. He screamed out, as if I hit him, and jumped away from where I'd let off.

"Oh my God, James," yelled Sandra. "Did he... are you hit?"

"Nah. Not this time. But let 'eem pull some shit like that again, he will be," I paused, "As you can see... I'm serious as fuck right na, Shonny. I swear on your life I will kill this bitch, you hear me?"

Shonny dropped to her knees and said, "I swear on my own life we don't know where he is."

I walked away from Sandra and approached Shonny. I tilted her head back to look in her eyes. She was telling the truth. I bit my bottom lip and my nostrils flared.

"Throw a rug over that lil' shit. No one will notice. Have a blessed night, family."

*

"What's the word, bro?" said Luck when he answered the phone.

"Come outside," I said before hanging up.

I opened the middle compartment to my car and fished around it for a Backwood and a jar of weed. I broke the Backwood down and dumped the ashes into the ashtray.

I was at Luck's crib after riding around all night trying to get a location on that nigga Dinero. Adrien and Juice had hit my line about a hundred times trying to link with me, but I wasn't with it. I didn't need a squad of incompetent ass niggas riding with me. What good would rolling around the city with a hundred niggas with me do for me? Absolutely nothing but irritate me further.

Luck hopped in the car and immediately took notice to my mood.

"I heard you went on a rampage on the block," he said as he scratched the back of his ear. "What chu on, famo?"

I huffed and shook my head, "I can't even say it."

I couldn't say that Dinero had raped Ryann out loud. Shit hurt me to my core... what hurt me even more was that she had shut me out. And for what? I knew she needed me right now.

I dragged my hand over the bottom portion of my face and sighed, "The Uber driver. I need that nigga to me pronto."

"Bodied?" asked Luck with raised eyebrows.

"Breathin," I replied with gritted teeth.

Luck nodded, "Ryann aight?"

I shook my head and snorted, "She will be, believe that, my nigga."

"Should I be worried, fam?"

"Only thing I need you to worry about is finding that nigga, cuz," I said as I stared off into space.

*

I sat in complete darkness, combing the nappy hairs on my beard. It was after four in the morning and I hadn't slept a wink. My mind wouldn't shut down. I wouldn't rest until I had that niggas head in my hands. I couldn't rest knowing that my shorty had be violated in ways that I never thought imaginable. Fuck was dawg on? Did he forgot about the gang of niggas running behind her? Aside from the gang of niggas backing baby, she had me.

I sighed and gripped the stress ball I was holding in my other hand. A stress ball I was given as a child. I still had it. It calmed me down when I was thinking irrationally. It calmed me down when I was thinking about doing some shit, like taking his whole bloodline out. It stopped me from unleashing this wrath on mafuckas who had nothing to do with this. Sometimes though, this stress ball didn't do its job. I learned that at a young age. Back when I stayed in the group home ran by Ms. Anne and Mr. Tyrone, when I slit Mr. Tyrone's throat.

After months of this nigga forcing me to do things no seven year old should be doing, I was about sick and tired of the nigga. He had me stealing and robbing mafuckas for his own gain. For food I wouldn't be able to touch. For juice, I would never be able to drink. That was the petty shit. I didn't truly reach my breaking point until he took shit too far.

I was eight. And she was ten. Mr. Tyrone was in his late forties. In this case though, his age meant nothing. What was of importance was the fact that he was supposed to take care of Beady and me. Instead, he did the opposite.

I always knew he was a sick mafucka. But when he basically forced me to watch him molest Beady, I knew for sure he was. Before he could finish fuckin on her, he sent me back to my room fuming, with my chest heaving up and down, balled fist, and flaring nostrils. He told me that he was trying to teach me how to fuck, but since I was unappreciative, I should go to my room and play with *'that ball that social worker ass bitch'* gave me.

I did. I went back to my room. I played with the stress ball. But it didn't calm me down. I was eight—I knew what was right and I knew what was wrong... and the sick shit he was doing? Shit was wrong. I kept envisioning the tears running down Beady's eyes. I kept hearing her cries for him to stop. I kept hearing her cry about how he was hurting her. And the stress ball... it didn't calm me down.

I thought rationally at first. I went to Ms. Anne. I did the right thing. I told her that her husband was having sex with Beady. Her response was for me to stay in a child's place and mind my own business before she made him fuck me too. I huffed. Fucked up, right? Her response did nothing but infuriate me further. I'd be damned if that nigga did to me what he was doing to her.

So... shit... I snuck off to the kitchen and grabbed one of the steak knives from the drawer. I crept down the hallway, down to the room he had her in... fucking her innocence away. I eased inside of the room and Mr. Tyrone was still heavily at it. He never saw me coming. Beady did. She laid on her back, silent now, in a daze. But when she saw me, there was a glimmer of hope that flashed across her face. I put my index finger up to my lips, telling her to remain quiet and she did. I crept behind Mr. Tyrone and quickly slit his throat.

Blood spilled from his throat and Beady quickly moved from up under him before he could fall on her. I grabbed her and held onto her trembling body. I told her everything was okay, but I knew she wouldn't be. Trauma like that is never easy to get over. I knew that Beady would never be the same after that. And I knew that I would never be the same either.

Mr. Tyrone turned me into a savage. I didn't know what he turned Beady into. I just knew she changed. And I wondered... if Ryann would change. I just wanted to be there for her the same way I was there for Beady. I just wanted to hold shorty and tell her that everything would be aight. Then... then I would catch the ho nigga Dinero and he would get the type of treatment Mr. Tyrone should have gotten. He was going to suffer fa sho.

The ringing of my phone snatched me out of my thoughts. I tossed the stress ball on the desk and answered my ringing phone.

"Yo," I answered.

"Found her," said Scotty before running Ryann's location down to me.

Chapter Two . Ryann

"Ryann, I don't think you should do this," said Omni as she pulled up in front of the abortion clinic.

"I didn't ask you what you thought, Omni," I replied as I unbuckled my seat belt.

As soon as I hung up with Goose, I called the abortion clinic to schedule an appointment. Since I had to wait forty-eight hours before I could come in, I stayed at a room downtown.

I didn't want to face anybody at this point and only called Omni because I would need a ride home. I didn't want to face anybody because of the conversation she and I were having. She didn't want me to get an abortion because she didn't agree with them. Well, I didn't either but that shit went right out of the window when I figured out that Dinero had raped me.

When I told her he raped me, she asked me if I was sure that had happened. I almost smacked the piss out of Omni. I just don't understand why some people think rape is only when someone holds you down and roughly forces themselves upon you. I told that nigga Dinero no. No means, no. I didn't give a fuck that we were in a relationship. He still forced himself on me. I was drunk, but I do remember trying to push him off me, and I do remember holding my legs closed which he pried apart. That shit was rape.

And it was my fault. I should have left him alone, a long time ago. I was so worried about him hurting himself and all I did was hurt myself in the process. I should have just left him. A red flag was raised when he put my gun to his head. I should have known that nigga was a straight up bitch. Instead, I let that dictate the way I handled him, when I should have let it dictate the way I handled my damn self.

"I'm just saying. Maybe you guys need to—

"Sometimes, I wonder why we're even best friends, Omni. I swear to God," I said as a ton of emotions washed over me.

Why did she think I should sit down with him? Why did we have to talk? I told her he raped me and her response was to talk it out. Because she didn't think it was rape. She thinks that I was just drunk and didn't know that I willingly had sex with him. I knew I didn't, because I had just told Cassim that I would never have sex with Dinero again. And I hadn't, which is why Dinero said that I was trying to keep it away from him. He hadn't fucked me because I wouldn't let him, so he took it.

"I'm sorry, Ry, please don't cry," she said as she unbuckled her seatbelt. "Listen, I truly do apologize. I'm not myself these days. Your brother just..."

There she goes... making this conversation about her and Juice's shit.

"Don't worry about it," I said as I got out of the car.

"I'm coming with you, Ry."

"Don't you have to work, Omniel?" I asked with an attitude.

I didn't want to sit up in this waiting room listening to her whine about how Juice was switching up and that she couldn't trust him. She shouldn't have trusted him to begin with. That nigga been dirty from the start.

"Yeah, I'll just call off," she replied as she unbuckled her seatbelt and killed the engine. "You need my support right now and I haven't been much of a good friend these days. I've been looking at your situation with judgment, when what I've should have been doing was being there for you. Like I always have been."

Omni was the supportive, caring, sweet best friend before she and Juice started to have problems. She was stressed but hell, that didn't mean turn into a bitch towards me. Whatever though. I was already going through shit and was not in the mood to argue with her. If she started that whining 'woe is me' shit I was just going to tune her out.

My phone rang and I looked around my purse for it. It was Cass. I did what I've been doing since yesterday—ignored him. I couldn't talk to him right now. I wouldn't. This baby could have been his and I was getting rid of it. Nine times out of ten, it was Dinero's and I just couldn't carry his baby. Something was seriously wrong with that mothafucka and I'd be damned if I risk my kid ending up with his fucked up DNA.

I sighed and stuffed the phone back into my purse.

"Who was that?" asked Omni, walking alongside of me.

"Cass."

"Did you tell him you were getting an abortion?" she asked.

"Hell no. I didn't even tell him I was pregnant," I said with an attitude as I pushed the door open.

I glanced at her and I could see that she wanted to say something, but she didn't. I shook my head and rolled my eyes, "This is my life, Om. Aight?"

She held her hands up, "I'm not saying anything, girl. Do you, baby, do you."

*

Four hours later, I was no longer pregnant.

I walked out of the back area and Omni was sitting in the waiting room, sleeping. I shook her awake and she wiped the sides of her mouth and sat up. She asked if I was okay and I nodded. If anything, I was emotionally distressed. Laying on that table, I thought about what I was doing and felt utterly disgusted with myself. I had to constantly remind myself that this was necessary. I had to. I couldn't be one of those bitches who didn't know who her baby daddy was. I couldn't stomach possibly being pregnant with Dinero's baby. The thought of the baby being his literally made me sick.

The whole ride back to the hotel room to get my things, I sat there in a daze while Omni talked about Juice. I sat there with my head rested against the window, thinking about Cass and how worried he had to be. He'd called me so many times and texted just as much. I couldn't talk to him right now. Not after I'd possibly just killed his kid. I needed some time to get myself together.

Not too long after, Omni was pulling up at the hotel, next to my car.

"Thank you, Om," I said, interrupting her whining.

"You're welcome. Please call your brothers; they've been on me heavy. Juice can tell when I'm lying and he knows that you were with me."

I frowned and asked, "Did you tell him about the abortion, Omniel?"

She sucked her teeth, "Of course not. What the hell?"

I told her I would call her later and hopped out of the car. I didn't know if it was my hormones or what but these days, Omni had been annoying the entire fuck out of me.

I walked into the hotel and got right on the elevator up to my room. My phone notification went off and I checked it.

Adri: Fuck you at, Ry?
Me: I'm okay. Will be there in an hr.

I sighed and stuffed my phone back into my purse. I looked down at the at home instructions I got from the abortion clinic and balled it up. I stuffed it down in the bottom of my purse and rested against the wall of the elevator looking up at the numbers.

What happened to the Dinero I knew before we got together? That nigga seemed to have it all together. Thinking back on how tight we were, and how cool he was, I would have never thought it. This nigga really raped me. He knew he was wrong too, because when I confronted him, he took off running. What the fuck is wrong with him? Did he forget about the squad of shooters that always had my back? Did he forget about the loose screws in Goose's head? He had to be out of his fuckin' mind to do something like that, knowing he would be done dirty over petty shit. Just imagine how my family is going to do him behind him raping me? Knowing Goose... shit's going to get real sick.

The elevator doors opened, and I headed down to my room. I looked around my purse for my room key, and unlocked to door when I got to it. Walking into the room, my phone rang, and I looked down into my purse to answer it.

"This what you do? You run? And shut me out? Where you been at all morning, Ry?"

My soul nearly jumped out of my damn body at the sound and sight of Cass sitting on the bed with his hands clasped together and a scowl on his face.

I swallowed and frowned, "How did you get into my room?"

He pushed himself up from the bed and treaded towards me with nothing but concern written on his face, "Come here."

I was shocked to see him open his arms to hug me. I just knew he was about to curse me the fuck out for ignoring his calls and going straight MIA. But he didn't. And since he didn't, I knew that he knew.

He grabbed hold of me and hugged me tightly. I closed my eyes, inhaling his scent, feeling the beat of his heart against my body, and felt better than I've felt in the past couple of days. He rubbed my back and told me that I should have told him.

"Don't shut me out, sweetheart," he softly said as he continued to hold and rub on me.

I silently wept as I held him tighter. I didn't want to let him go. I wanted this feeling to last forever. There was nothing on earth that made me feel the way Cassim made me feel. I had been having a horrible day until I was in his arms. Until his manly scent crept up my nostrils. Cassim's scent was the sweetest aroma therapy. It was all I needed to get through a tough time. In this moment, Dinero raping me didn't matter. The abortion didn't matter. The only thing that mattered was that I was finally in his arms. The only thing that mattered was that I heard his voice. The raspy, deep, panty wetting voice of Cassim.

"I didn't," I finally replied after about three minutes of silence and just standing there in his embrace.

He tried to pull away and I held onto him tighter.

"Don't," I said.

Cassim kissed me on the forehead, "This nigga... straight violated my fuckin baby."

He was sad. I hated that he was sad. I hated to see that look in his eyes. Like he was hopeless. Like there was nothing he could do to make me feel better. For him to feel like he was hopeless, hurt me. A man so strong. So, big, so powerful... but in this moment, he felt hopeless. I never wanted him to feel that way.

"It's... it's okay."

He didn't say anything. He just wrapped his arms tighter around me, like he never wanted to let me go. I stood there, with my ear pressed against him, listening to the fast pace of his heart rate, and the heaviness of his breathing. His body was trembling, he was so upset. And I wondered if he was mad because he didn't know? Because I had disappeared

"You mad at me," I asked, with a voice slightly muffled by his shirt.

"You scared me sweetheart. That's it," he paused and pulled me away from his chest to look me in the eyes. "Mad at you? Nah, baby. I'm mad at myself.'

"Mad at yourself? Why?"

He looked away and then just pulled me back into his arms.

"Cassim…"

He sighed and scratched the tip of his nose, "If I would have really made you leave that nigga a long time ago? None of this shit even would have happened. True enough.. you's a grown ass woman, Ryann, but if I would have been a lil' mo persuasive… you would have left the pussy nigga. Nothing any of us doin' to him will erase the fuck shit he did and baby… that shit eats at me."

I wrapped my arms around his neck and said, "Cassim… I was afraid to leave him because when I tried to, he put a gun to his head. So no, this is not your fault. It is mine. I cared too much about what he would do if I left him. I should have stayed away from him, but after Peewee got shot, I tried to be there for him. I didn't think," I looked off and shook my head. "I didn't think Dinero could do that to me."

I truly didn't. Who rapes someone they love? What kind of animal? He couldn't have loved me as much as he said he did. I think Dinero just wanted to keep me. He didn't want to lose me. As I said before, I was like a prize to most of these niggas simply because I'm a Mosley, and not too many mafuckas can say they had me. So, I felt like maybe Dinero didn't want to lose me. Especially not to Cass—the type of dude I said I would never fall for. Dinero was intimidated and knew that he was losing me. If he truly loved me, he would have just let me go.

"He's a weak ass nigga. A true ass pussy," said Cassim fuming. "Those type of niggas... sucka ass... weak minded ass lil' boys? They can't be trusted. Shit you should've let 'eem put that bullet in his dome. Fuck 'em. No mercy for niggas like that."

I didn't say anything. I just stood there, hugging him. Wondering how he'd feel about me if he knew I just had an abortion. I was never going to tell him that.

I wouldn't have to though.

Remember how I said life had a fucked up sense of humor?

*

"Goose," I said as I stood in the doorway of the living room, watching him sitting, unmoving in the middle of the living room floor. He sat there, in the middle of the floor, cracking up, in the dark surrounded by guns damn near bigger than me.

It was almost two in the morning and the house was empty with the exception of us two. I was scared shitless. Although I knew that it was Dinero that Goose was after, I was still petrified. I should have called Juice because Goose was out of his mind. It was the first anybody had seen him since I called him with the news.

He quickly glanced over his shoulder at me, "Yo, wassup baby sis. You aight? You need somethin'?"

"You okay?" I asked, taking slow steps into the dimly lit living room. On top of the guns surrounding him, he had candles surrounding him too like he was on some black magic type of shit. The loud sound of his laughter, and yelling, is what drew me out of my sleep.

"Yeah, Ry baby," he shouted before quickly jumping up. He moved his head from side to side, cracking the bones in his neck.

"What are you doing?" I asked steady inching into the living room.

He smiled widely, like a lunatic. The glow from the candles shining on his face made him look like something straight out of a horror film. I couldn't take too much more of this shit and felt along the wall for a light switch. When I turned it on, I gasped and covered my mouth with my hands.

"Turn it off," he coldly demanded.

"What...What did you do, Goose?" I asked as tears poured from my eyes.

"I asked for Dinero. They wouldn't give him to me," he said as he began to rock side to side.

Goose was shirtless and covered in blood. His face, his body, his hands, the blue jean shorts he wore, the black Lebron's he had on, hell there was even blood in his hair.

I hurried past him, jumping over tea light candles in the process to look out of the window. Blue and Red lights flickered about the neighborhood, and I could see a few ambulances, and police cars down the block.

"What did you do," I screamed as I backed away from the window.

"What was necessary. Now, leave me to my repentance, Ryann."

I took off to my bedroom where I quickly grabbed my phone and called Juice.

He answered immediately, "What's up?"

"Something.. Goose did something."

I was so scared that I was shaking.

"He's there?"

"Yes... I don't... I don't know how long he will be though."

"Calm down, Ry. I'm on the way."

I didn't want to be here. I wanted to leave. I needed Cassim's arms around me. I needed him to tell me that it would be alright. What had Goose done? Who's blood did he have on him? Oh God, I prayed he hadn't killed Shonny and the parents. Please, God.

They had nothing to do with it. They didn't deserve to be murdered. Standing in my room, shaking like a leaf on a tree, I thought back to my parents murder. My mother had nothing to do with whatever beef Lesley had with my dad, but he killed her too. Guilty by association. Is that what just happened to Shonny and she and Dinero's parents?

I cracked my bedroom door open and jumped back at the sight of Goose standing right in front of it.

"I'm sorry, Ryann," he apologized with his head down, his voice dripping with sadness like a disobedient child.

His mood was all over the place. He'd gone from straight monstrous to the disposition of a child. I didn't know if I should have hugged Goose or if I should have ran. So instead, I just stood there looking up at him. After about ten seconds, he walked away heading for the backdoor. Glancing out into the living room I saw that he had cleaned the candles up and put the guns away.

As soon as he was out of the house, I jetted to the window to see what was going on down the street. There were people in the street crying and falling out.

I swallowed a knot in my throat as I slowly made my way to the front door. What did Goose do? I twisted the doorknob, and the moment the door was slightly cracked I could hear the screams. They taunted me to a point where I had to slam the door close.

What had he done?

*

"Who did he kill," I asked Juice, as I sat on the couch biting at my nails.

Minutes felt like hours as I sat in this dark house, watching the red and blue lights flicker on my walls, waiting for my brothers to get here. I didn't know where Goose had gone. I didn't know what he had done. I knew whatever he had done was horrible and gruesome because that is just the way he did shit. Sometimes Goose was like a big cuddly teddy bear, and other times he was like a big, scary, monster. Other times happened more than some times.

"Whole family," he said as he scratched at his head. "'Cept Peewee."

"Had he been there, that lil' nigga would've gotten the same work," said Adri as he cleaned his Buffs with a microfiber rag.

It blew the fuck out of me how these niggas were sitting here, nonchalant like Goose didn't just kill three innocent people.

"And y'all," I paused and huffed. "Y'all just don't give a fuck huh?"

"Why would we?" asked Juice with a frown of confusion on his face. "Now maybe that nigga Dinero will show his face."

"Soons he do," Adri paused, put his arm up, and pulled the trigger to an imaginary gun. "Pop! Blowin' that bitch clean off. You hear me?"

Juice leaned forward and picked his phone up from the table, "Shid bruh... not if G get to 'eem first."

"What chu crying for, Ry," asked Adrien, taking notice to the tears streaming down my face.

I locked eyes with him, "Didn't you care about Shonny? She...Goose killed her...and you don't care?"

Adrien fucked with Shonny on the regular. Yet, he sat there cleaning the lens to his glasses like nothing had happened. My brothers. My brothers. My brothers... How could they be so heartless? They were emotionally detached from everything and everybody but me. I couldn't really explain it but I felt selfish in a sense.

Adrien shook his head, "Nah. I don't."

I pushed myself up from the couch and stormed off towards the room. Juice grabbed my arm as I passed by him.

"I would put a bullet through the middle of Omni's face if—

"Stop," I yelled as I snatched away from him.

I didn't want to hear it. Hearing it would make me think it, and I didn't want to imagine losing Omni.

"I'm going to bed," I said as I continued to my room.

"We just love you, Ry baby. It's all love, sis," said Adrien before I slammed my bedroom door closed.

*

I sighed as I stared at my reflection in the mirror, expressionless. Every passing moment was spent thinking about everything that had transpired over the past few days. I was stressed and sad.

Knock. Knock.

"Ry, you woke," asked Nek from the other side of the door.

"Mmhmm," I replied as I grabbed my hot flat irons from the vanity.

Nek walked into my room and immediately hugged me, "I'm so sorry, Ryann."

I didn't want her arms around me. The only arms I wanted around me were Cassim's. He was the only thing that made a smile slide across my face. I couldn't wait for him to pick me up in a few.

"Sorry about what," I said as my arms laid flat to my sides.

When she realized that I just wasn't into the hug, she pulled away with a sigh.

"For what happened, Ryann," she said with her hands stuffed into the back pockets of her booty shorts. "Do you think he still would have did that if you were still fucking him?"

I narrowed my eyes at her, pushed myself up from the vanity, and stood up, "What you sayin' Shaneka?"

She took a step back, "I'm just saying… if you would have kept fucking him… maybe he wouldn't have raped you… then you wouldn't have had to tell Goose and set that nigga off. Now… now three people are—

Whamp!

I punched Shaneka in the face and she crashed against my vanity, knocking all of my shit over. I couldn't believe she had come on me like that! I would have expected some dumb shit like that to come out of Ashlee's mouth. The both of them had been acting mad shady since all of this shit went down. It was like I didn't have anybody but Cass and my brothers in my corner.

What kind of brains do the bitches I hang with have? I told that nigga no. I'm not obligated to give my pussy to nan' nigga but these bitches feel like I was? They think I should have kept fucking him? Omni was acting funny as hell too, talking about was I sure he raped me.

While LeeLee running her dick suckers talking about I just want attention.

When the fuck ever has Ryann been thirsty for attention? I gets that shit with little to no effort. I was dead ass hurt. I couldn't believe my peoples were treating me this way, when I needed them the most.

Shaneka regained her composure before coming at me with wild arms. I grew up with three brothers, I didn't do that wind milling shit. I straight squared up with bitches. So, when Nek thought that was going to fly with me, I dodged all them lil' petty hits and punched her in the face again.

A few seconds later, my bedroom door was pushed open and in came Ashlee. She yelled, "Ryann what the fuck are you doing—"

"What the fuck am I doing?" I asked, breathing heavily, pointing at my heaving chest. "This bitch... this bitch came in here with that stupid talking shit! Low key, you can get this work too! I don't have time for it, aight?! Miss me with it! If any one of you bitches say another fuckin' slick thing to me, you hos will be on the streets. Or back in that hot ass crib on the west side. Keep playing with me!"

"Come on, Nek," said Ashlee with a deep scowl on her face. "Bitch you need a chill pill. Go take some pictures or suck some dick or something. You need to check ya self."

Did these hos forget what I just went through? Maybe the experience was so traumatic to me because I had to get an abortion. Only Omni knew that though. Still, without that knowledge, my cousins could have been there for me a lot more than what they were. I never expected that out of Nek. She was usually always supportive and sweet. But these days, the bitch had switched up.

They hurried out of my room and I sat my ass right back down at my vanity to get ready.

*

"Cass... do you know her?" I asked Cassim as I nodded at the dark skin lady standing in front of the store, staring as we headed to his car.

I was finally with my baby and I was in a good mood. I couldn't wait to get out of that house with them bitches. They were mad and sitting on the porch passing a blunt back and forth when Cass pulled up. They were green with envy too.

Aside from getting away from Ashlee and Shaneka, I wanted to get away from the hood period. It was depressing. Everybody knew what happened was because of something Dinero did, and they knew that somehow I was involved. Instead of thinking that Goose did it though, they thought Cass did. Apparently, he went down to Dinero's people house cutting up trying to find him.

People knew how Cass got down though, and torturing wasn't his thing. He'd rather put a bullet through a niggas head and get it over with. But what Goose did... it was sick and twisted. He left all of their bodies without eyes. Knowing Goose, he dug them out while they were still breathing. In addition to their eyes being missing, their nails and nail beds had been removed as well as their tongues. They suffered. They suffered bad before he gutted them like fish.

Cass glanced over his shoulder and sighed deeply, I glanced too and this time she was smiling and waving.

"Who is that?" I asked, as I stood there waiting for him to open the door for me.

"Nobody," he quickly replied.

But the flaring of his nostrils, and the insane grip he had on the door, told me he knew her and he wasn't happy to see her. Cass chewed on his bottom lip and told me to get in after I'd been standing there staring into those cold black eyes of his.

I shook my head and slid into the car. We'd loaded up on junk food and were on our way to his house. He wanted to take me out to eat, but I told him all I wanted to do was lie up under him all day with his phone on silent. He was a little hesitant about the whole silent phone thing, but eventually he gave in because I'm Ryann... duh!

Cass got in and tossed the bag of junk food in my lap, "Here fatty."

"The only thing fat on me is this ass... and this monkey," I joked.

He laughed and pulled his seatbelt on. I followed suit and dug into the grocery bag.

Knock. Knock. Knock.

My soul damn near jumped out of my body at the sound of someone knocking on my window. I turned to look and it was the old, dark skin woman. Up close, I could see that she'd had a hard life. She had craters in her face, and she was missing teeth. She was a fiend for sure.

"You got fiends just walking up to the car now?" I said with an attitude.

"Cassim! Cassim! Come... come talk to me, baby," said the woman as she slapped on the window.

I turned to Cassim with my head slightly cocked. He kept his eyes straight ahead with a deadly grip on the steering wheel. This lady wasn't trying to buy drugs. This lady knew Cass personally. She had to. I'm sure he didn't go around giving just anybody his government name. He was so bothered by her presence that it saddened and worried me.

I touched his arm and he quickly flinched away before snatching his seatbelt off.

"Are you ok—"

He hopped out of the car and slammed the door before I could ask if he was okay. I sat there fumbling with the unopened back of Hot Flamin' Cheetos, wondering what the hell he was going to do to the lady. She looked scared herself, as she timidly backed away from the car with her shaky skinny hands out.

I watched as Cassim stood in front of her with his hands stuffed into his front pockets, slightly leaning forward, speaking to her with tight lips. She looked up at him with wide eyes and a trembling lip. Cassim scratched at his dreads and angrily walked off, while the lady stood there with tears falling from her eyes, watching him.

He got back into the car and I asked him what was said. He told me nothing before speeding away from the curb.

The rest of the ride to his house was silent.

Chapter Three . Cass

"Cassim! Cassim," I woke up to Ryann shoving me with a concerned look on her face.

"What? Wassup," I groggily asked as I pulled her down onto my chest. "You aight, sweetheart?"

She looked up at me with sad eyes, "You were crying in your sleep."

She reached up and wiped just under my eye before showing me her wet fingertips. I closed my eyes and wrapped my arms around her body. She asked me if I was alright and I told her to go to sleep. It had been over ten years since I cried in my sleep. Hell, it had been about ten years since I had the dream she had waken me out of. Shit was most likely triggered by seeing 'her' yesterday.

When I was about eight, I started having these reoccurring dreams about a perfect life. Everything was smooth. I had loving parents, food to eat, water to drink, I was in school... you know, the normal shit kids living in a stable household had. Everything was gravy. Until one day, I came home from school to nothing.

The white walls turned black, the nice marble floors began to deteriorate to damaged hardwood, the nice ass furniture that sat in the living room crumbled up, all of the food in the refrigerator began to mold. The water stopped working. Rats, mice, and roaches began to infest the house. Everything just went to shit. The nice clothes I had on, turned to rags. The shoes on my feet, shrunk four sizes too small, and I went from being able to speak, to not being able to say a damn word.

And then she came home. Not the nice, clean young woman I dreamt about. It was the crackhead bitch who always referred to me as mothafucka.

She staggered into the crib and threw an already open pack of bologna across the room at me. It slid across the floor and hit me in the knee, "Here, mothafucka. Eat up."

She'd leave right after and I'd be left alone.

I didn't want to be left alone. The house was dark and scary. I was cold and hungry. I wanted a mother. I wanted a family. But I had no one.

That dream fucked with me for years. I didn't stop having them until I was about eighteen.

I felt like a sucka ass nigga, whimpering and shit in my sleep, but some things are out of our control. One of the things I appreciated most about Ryann was when I was uncomfortable about something, she didn't press me for answers. There was still so much shorty didn't know about me, but that didn't stop her from loving me.

She lifted her head from my chest and looked me in the eyes, "I love you."

I was caught off guard. Shorty ain't never told me she loved me. I knew she did, but she's never let he words come out of her mouth. I've never said those words to anybody, not ever so I said nothing. I kissed her on the forehead and said, "I know, sweetheart."

I could tell that wasn't the response she was looking for, but she didn't get on me about it. She laid her head back on my chest and a few minutes later, I felt her tears wetting up my chest.

I lifted her head up and stared into her eyes, "You know I feel the same way about you, right?"

"Uh huh," she replied before running her tongue over her bottom lip.

The words she wanted to hear were caught up in my throat. I wanted to say it, but shit, I couldn't.

*

"Call that nigga Juice," I told Luck as I stared at Dinero laid out on his stomach on top of an old table Luck tied him to before I got here.

"Already did, famo. I'll let 'eem know you touched down though," He said as he fished his phone from his pocket.

Right after I dropped Ryann off at the crib, Juice hit my line and told me he had eyes on the pussy nigga Dinero. Dawg was in the process of buying a plane ticket when Luck snatched him the fuck up outta there. Now we were posted up at an abandoned clinic we use to leave niggas leaking at, in its basement about to do work.

As agreed between the Mosley's and I, whoever found the nigga first was to let the other party know. I wanted Dinero to myself, but since I'm a man of my word, I'll share this nigga with 'em.

I snatched my burner from my waistband as I approached bitch boy with gritted teeth. I had never wanted to body a nigga so badly in my life. I've never been the torturing type of cat, but with this nigga... I wanted to make it hurt.

I stood at the table and took notice to the baseball bat sitting a few feet away from me. I smirked and stuffed my burner back into my waistband. I picked the bat up, and wrapped my hand around it before bringing it down over his ankles.

"Ahhhhhhhh," he screamed, waking his stupid ass the fuck up. "Where... where am I?"

I maneuvered around the table so that he could get a good look at me. When he did, his eyeballs nearly popped out of socket. I kneeled in his face and smiled, "Your final destination."

He began to squirm, trying to free himself from the table, but the nigga was wasting his time. Luck had him tied down with chains.

I gripped the baseball bat and brought it down over the heel of his foot, breaking it on impact.

"Them niggas—fuck bro," said Luck heading my way. "Shittttt."

"What they say," I asked as I brought the baseball bat down over his other foot.

"They on the way."

"Betta hope this nigga breathing when they get here," I said before bringing the bat down over his back.

Crack! The sound of the bones in his back breaking was slightly muffled by his screams. But the shit was like music to my ears. Every time I thought about how the pussy nigga violated my heart, I got madder every time. This nigga deserved everything I was inflicting on him plus more.

I gritted my teeth and raised the bat up, getting ready to bring it down over his head but Luck stopped me, "The agreement, fam."

I shook my shoulder away from him, "Nigga, what? Fuck the agreement. Do you know what this puss ass nigga did to my shorty?"

"I—I sorry," cried Dinero.

"Come on, bro," pled Luck.

My nostrils flared as I brought it down over the side of his face instead, twisting his jaw up like a pretzel.

"Aaaaaaaah," he yelled.

I dropped the bat and said, "Tell me when they get here, nigga."

I walked off and headed up the stairs, fishing around my pocket for a blunt with shaky hands. I wanted to kill the nigga. I didn't give a fuck about an agreement, didn't give a fuck about the consequences behind killing him before the Mosley's touched down either. But respect is respect, and if I give a mafucka my word, I stick to it.

Difference in this situation was that this nigga deserved to die like...right fuckin na. Weak ass, goofy ass nigga, yo. I was heated, leaning up against the kitchen wall, busting a Backwood down, with gritted teeth. I chewed on my bottom lip as I continued to bust it down.

A couple minutes later, Luck joined me upstairs with a jar of weed.

"What he do, boss?" he asked.

I looked up at him with eyes as narrow as slits, and a twitching top lip.

"Bitch nigga violated Ry, bruh?" he asked, continually egging shit on like he couldn't tell that I didn't want to talk about the shit.

"Stop talkin' Luck."

I was trying to keep a cool head. I was trying not to go down stairs and jam that bat down his throat. So, it was definitely a bad time for Luck to be bringing what Dinero did up.

Luck handed me the jar of weed and rested against the wall next to me, "What's understood ain't gotta be explained, famo."

*

About five minutes had passed before the Mosley's and their squad were banging on the front door. I slapped hands with every one of them except Goose. That nigga came rushing through the crib like a raging bull. He sent me a quick what up and hurried down the stairs. I didn't take it personal because that's just how the nigga is.

We all jogged down the stairs behind him, exchanging a few words. They wanted to prolong the niggas death. Wanted to do shit like, stick needles underneath his fingernails, burn 'em with shit... you know, torture. I was all for making the nigga suffer, but what I wasn't with was what that nigga Goose was doing when we got to the bottom of the stairs.

"Yoo, what's with this shit," I yelled, as I pointed sideways at Goose who was ramming the baseball bat up Dinero's ass.

This nigga Goose was off into some ol' other shit. Dawg was forcefully ramming the same baseball bat I'd just broke Dinero's jaw with, up his ass. We were about twenty miles from the nearest neighbor, but I still felt like this niggas screams could be heard by 'em.

Juice lit the blunt he was handling, took a few pulls from it and shrugged, "Let 'eem work."

"You niggas getting a kick outta watchin' this nigga butt fuck another man with a baseball bat?" I asked as my eyes scanned the crowd of about twenty niggas, they brought with them, attentively watching the shit go down.

"That nigga right there," said Loc pointing at Dinero. "He violated the queen so it's only right that he gets violated too, my nigga."

"The queen," I asked with a snort. "*My* queen. Stop talkin' that queen shit when it comes to my shorty, Loc, before I toss ya bitch ass on top of that table next to that nigga."

He ran his tongue over his bottom lip with a smirk, "Aight, Cass. Aight. You talkin' greasy."

"Greasy and factual, G," I said with a mug as I treaded towards the pool table.

I wasn't with that twisted type shit. I liked to inflict pain on a mafucka, and that's exactly what I had planned for 'em. But this shit here? Shit was straight faggotty to me.

"Be easy, nigga. That's just how this nigga refers to her," said Juice extending the blunt to me.

"Referred. It's over for that shit, bruh," I replied as I declined the blunt.

I was on a mission. I wasn't about to sit back smoking weed while this nigga butt fucked Dinero.

When Goose noticed me coming his way, he stopped ramming the bat up Dinero's ass with a pause.

"Let me get a piece of this goofy, my nigga," I said with my hand extended.

Goose smiled wide and hopped his big crazy ass down from the table, thinking I was really about to finish the butt fucking. The smile he once wore, was quickly replaced with his infamous mug as he stood alongside me with his arms crossed over his chest.

"Puh-please.... Please..." whimpered Dinero as he laid there with blood spilling from his ass.

I frowned and looked away as I pulled the bat out of his ass.

"Don't—Don't—

Before he could get another word out, I jumped on top of the table and hit him in the back of his head with the bat.

"Fuck is you doin' nigga," yelled Goose with a deep scowl on his face. "I'm not finished with him yet," he said in a low, deep, demonic tone.

That nigga was on another level of crazy. But I really wasn't here for the looney tune type shit. If this nigga wanted to bitch about me murking Dinero before he could finish fuckin' em, then so be it. It is what it is. If these niggas want prol'lems we can go there too.

"Peep game, bruh," I said before pinching the bridge of my nose. "That faggotty shit... not happenin. I got this pussy here. And if I don't want 'eem fucked... he won't be fucked. Dig me, G?"

"I'm not gonna fuck the nigga, C. Let me at 'em before he stops breathin at least. FUCK," Goose yelled.

I nodded and handed him the bat. He snatched it from my hands and then kindly asked me if I could hop off the table, "I'm not ready for him to die. Let me have a lil bit of fun before you dip 'em."

I nodded and jumped down from the table. Goose dropped the bat on the table, then fished around his pockets for something. A couple of seconds later, Juice and Adrien joined us at the table.

"I don't even know why you let this nigga at him first, bro," mumbled Adrien to Juice. "It's gone take a small army to shut him off."

"I'll handle Goose. Don't worry about it," said Juice before passing the blunt to Adrien.

These niggas were talking about Goose like he was a true ass animal. I looked up at him standing over Dinero, with a box cutter in his hand. He kneeled down and turned Dinero's head to the side.

"Fuckin' slicing this niggas eyelids off," said Adrien sounding choked up from the blunt.

I moved around the table to see if what Adrien said Goose was doing was legit. Sure, as shit, when I got a good look at the scene, that's exactly what this fuckin' nigga was doing. Straight savage shit. Artistic, psychopathic type of shit.

I snorted with a chuckle, "You on ya surgical shit huh, G?"

Goose gave me a quick glance over his shoulder a menacing smirk on his face, "I want him to see it."

"See what," I asked with a frown. "Yo, how much longer you gone be? I'm trying to end this nigga right now, and you wanna play."

"I want him to see it coming," he said. "Just give me a fuckin' minute!"

I looked over my shoulder at Juice and Adrien, "Ayo, control this situation."

Juice nodded and scratched at the tip of his and treaded towards us, "Aight G. Let me at 'em. You had enough fun with the nigga, boss."

Goose didn't say anything. He moved his head from side to side and went back to removing Dinero's other eyelid. You would think that the pussy nigga would have been dead from the brutal blow I gave him to the back of his head, but he wasn't. Shit was split, and leaking, for sure though. He was conscious, feeling everything that Goose was inflicting on him. Fuck was this nigga? Immortal? He should have passed out from the pain a long time ago. His screams were echoing through the fairly empty basement. His screams were the only sound filling the room. Everybody was silent. Everybody was straight buggin off the work this crazy nigga was putting in.

"Goose—

"He ain't hearing you, G," I said with a sneer.

These niggas wanted to handle him with care. But me... I didn't give a fuck about all 'lat. I wanted this shit over, this shit was about to be over. I had a nice lil' bath waiting on Dinero and I wanted him alive for it. I wasn't sure of how much life Goose was leaving in him, so the shit was deaded.

I grabbed Goose by the tail of his shirt and snatched him off the table. He went tumbling back into his brothers.

"Luck," I yelled, ignoring the gang of niggas looking like they wanted to snatch my head clean off my shoulders.

No fucks were giving. The Mosley's were holding Goose back. He was like a raging bull, wanting at me. It took Juice, Adrien, and Loc to hold him back. I was unbothered, unchaining Dinero from the table.

Luck treaded over and flicked a blunt tail from his hand before kneeling next to me, "Shit was turning into the Goose show wasn't it fam?"

I snorted, "Fuck 'em." I looked up over at them, "Calm down, bruh."

Goose was raging mad. I couldn't help but crack up laughing at the growling and shit he was doing. Shit was straight comical to me. I let this nigga butt fuck Dinero... let 'em slice his fuckin' eyelids off and all lat. He got his rocks off. Didn't even let his other brothers inflict any pain on him. Dawg was selfish with his bodies. Shit, I was too. But a deal is a deal.

I pulled Dinero down from the table by his leg and he hit the cement flooring of the basement with a loud thud. As I dragged him across the basement, I pointed at the Mosley's with my freehand, "Yo, y'all want to get a lil' work in before I dip this nigga?"

"Dip 'eem," said Loc with a frown. "Fuck you talm'bout—

"I'm not talkin to you, Loc. Shits not for you to understand."

Loc piped down. He fucked with the Mosleys, but the nigga was on my payroll. He was a hitter. Use to roll with Chicago and them, but since Chicago was a memory, Loc was pretty much running that team now. It was my money that kept him laced in Buffs and designer, so he shut the fuck up and proceeded to holding Goose's big mad ass back.

"Nah dawg... just do what you gotta do to get this nigga the fuck gone," said Juice.

Nigga was dead ass mad because his big stupid ass brother had ruined the experience for them.

I shrugged and proceeded to dragging Dinero, with the whole squad of mafuckas following behind me. I heard the whispers. I heard them talking amongst each other. Wondering what the fuck I meant by dipping him.

Finally, we stopped at the huge tub of sulfuric acid.

I wasted no time tossing that nigga inside. Alive, and screaming.

Satisfaction. That's what the fuck I felt.

Chapter Four . Ryann

It was after midnight when my brothers came barging into my bedroom like lunatics. I was up though. Lately, I hadn't been able to sleep much. The shit I've been through, and the things I've done, had been haunting me like never before. I wasn't sure if I'd ever be able to get a good night's rest again.

Knock. Knock.

"Ry, you up?" I heard Adrien say in the darkness.

"Yeah," I replied, sitting up straight.

Seconds later, the bedroom light was turned on. Adrien, Goose, and Juice all stood in my bedroom, by the front door, looking at me.

I frowned, "What's wrong?"

They came further into the room and sat at the foot of my bed.

"We never got a chance to apologize to you," said Juice with dipped eyebrows and regret in his eyes.

"Apologize for what? Yo, you niggas are dead ass creeping me out."

Goose snorted and gripped the tip of his nose, "For not protecting you the way we should have. From this point on, niggas will be under heavy scrutiny. Nobody touches you—

"Whoa, calm down," I said with my hands raised. "I'm in a relationship with Cass, all of you know that. And you all also know that, that nigga will raise hell for me."

Adrien nodded, "Cass is aight. Dawg came through in the clutch. Stay with that nigga forever. Because listen," he poked me in the bottom of my feet as he talked, "the next nigga? He won't get in. We were too lenient with that fuck nigga Dinero."

I giggled because these niggas were dead ass telling me that I wasn't allowed to date anybody but Cassim. I mean, that's all fine and dandy, since I'm going to be his wife anyway but still... I felt like they were bugging. Not everyone is as sick as Dinero.

"What do you mean he came through in the clutch?" I asked, purposely ignoring that they were trying to control who I associated myself with.

It was going to go deeper than just dating. I know this, because I know my brothers. Any guy I associate myself with is going to be given hell.

Juice scratched the back of his neck, "Don't even—

"That nigga," said Goose interrupting Juice, pointing at me with a huge grin on his face. "He found Dinero." He stopped smiling. His nostrils flared, and the veins in his neck popped out. "He blessed me with that nigga." He moved his head and shoulders around with closed eyes, "I can still hear his screams. He... he didn't expect me to fuck him in the ass with that bat—

"Yooooo," said Adrien, jumping up from the bed. "Bruh, tame this nigga."

Juice laid on his back, across my bed with his eyes on the ceiling, "Goose, be chill. Ryann don't need the details. All she need to know is that the nigga was handled."

A cool chill ran down my spine when I locked eyes with Goose. I wondered, how on earth could he be as cuddly as a teddy bear at times, but as scary as the devil himself during others? He terrified me. With the face of my daddy, but with the soul and heart of lucifer. How? How did my parents breed such savages? And not with just my brothers... with me too.

I was just as bad. I had to be, because I sat there satisfied with a smile on my face. Happy that Dinero had gotten what he'd gotten.

*

Two weeks later
"Bitch, you see that fine ass chocolate nigga standing in line with the dreads," said one of the ho's behind me.

I stood on my tiptoes to see who the two hood rats standing behind me were talking about, and was surprised to see Cass standing in line holding lingerie.

"Yes bitch. He's holding panties and shit, so he might have a girlfriend."

"Tuh! When the fuck have I ever cared? I nigga snatch all day, every day," she said before slapping hands with her girl.

I moved my bang out of my face and turned around, "Try it. Please, sweetie. If you think for one second that you can snatch my nigga from me... Try to snatch 'em. Pleeeease," I said with a smile on my face.

She drew back, "Of course he'll flex and front since you in here, ho."

"He don't even know I'm here, my baby," I told her matter-of-factly.

Cassim didn't know I was in here. He didn't even know I was at the mall. I came here because his birthday was in a few days and I wanted to cop something sexy for him. A few weeks had passed and I was finally in good spirits. I was at the mall with Omni, LeeLee, and Nek.

Things pretty much went back to normal when I got home from Cassim's the next day. Shaneka apologized about what she said and Ashlee did too. They gave some bullshit excuse behind their insensitivity and I just nodded to keep shit copacetic. Drama has never been my thing. I knew they were being fake, and that that 'we didn't realize that nonconsensual sex is like... basically rape' excuse made absolutely no sense. I could take that excuse from a bone head like Ashlee, but Nek knows what the hell rape is.

The girl smiled and said, "Don't be mad when he check for my bad ass."

Yeah, she was bad. Thick ass red bone, tatted, with inches down to her phat ass. The type of broad that could snatch niggas from bitches. But my nigga is different. He worshipped the ground I walked on. Yeah, he worshipped the ground I walked on, but when I told him I loved him he didn't say anything in return. I've been trying not to let that affect my attitude towards him, but I'd be lying if I said I was unaffected by it. I could tell that he loved me by his actions, but damn, it'd be nice to hear it. Since that night, I haven't brought up love or him crying in his sleep, although it's happened two more times since then.

It scared the hell out of me, but instead of bringing it up, all I'd do was hold him and tell him it would be alright. He would still be asleep, but in a way, it soothed him, and I was happy with that. Consoling him without his knowledge was a lot easier than doing it while he was awake.

After all of this time, Cassim was still a little guarded when it came to his past. I knew he was an orphan and that's about it. He hadn't shared anything about his childhood with me. There was so much that I wanted to know, like who that dark skin woman was, and why he was so bothered by her presence. I wanted to ask about the crying in his sleep, but strong men like Cassim are to be handled with care. Kind of like Goose, but shit, Cass was nowhere near on the same level of crazy as him.

"Don't cry when ya nigga ask for my sister number," said the other girl.

I was playing a dirty game, and this whole thing could go, left but I was confident. Cassim didn't have eyes for anyone but me. Whenever we were together, his undivided attention was on Ryann. Difference now is that he don't know I'm standing right behind him "I'm not worried," I said as my foot impatiently tapped against the floor.

I watched as Cass stood there, with his head slightly cocked to the side, facing straight ahead. Shorty was standing slightly in front of him, to the left because there was someone in line in front of Cass so she couldn't stand directly in front of him. She played in her hair, smiled, and even touched him.

The only thing Cass responded to was her touch and it wasn't the way she wanted.

"Yo, shorty. I know you or something," he paused and shifted his weight from one leg to the other. "Keep ya hands to yourself, darling."

She said a few hushed words to him, steady flirting, but Cass stuffed his free hand in his pocket and told her he was uninterested. She glanced over to where I was standing and said, "You frontin' cause yo girl in here? Nigga, if she wasn't you would be all over this phat ass. Stop playin!"

Cass looked over his shoulder and snatched his buff's off his face. He had a frown on his face as he approached me. He hated shit like this, so I'm mad the bitch felt salty enough to call me out. Most of the people in the front of the store were watching us. Cassim hated attention; especially negative, drama filled attention.

He walked away from the girl and headed in my direction. My pussy pulsated with every step he took. He was so damn fine when he was mad. His thick eyebrows were dipped, and just a hint of anger was in his eyes. It didn't matter how mad Cassim got at me, I could always see a glimmer of love in his eyes.

I smiled a little and took a few steps in his direction.

"You think shit cute?" he asked as he pulled me into his arms and firmly gripped my ass.

"Yep. I told her she was wasting her time."

Cassim pressed his forehead against mine and I stood on my tiptoes a bit to kiss him on his lips. Just like that, that little bit of anger he had was washed away. He bit on my bottom lip before pulling away from the kiss.

"Ugh, y'all so extra," said LeeLee, walking up with Omni, and Nek.

I rolled my eyes, "And ho, you so jealous." I looked around the store and as expected the hoodrat and her sister was looking. "Just like the rest of these bitches."

"Be chill," said Cassim, with his hand steady firmly holding onto my ass cheek.

"I thought we were supposed to be having a girl's day," said Nek with an attitude.

What the fuck was up with these two bitches attitudes? The only one who seemed to be cordial and sweet was Omniel. Shaneka and Ashlee were blowing the hell out of me, and if it wasn't for Cass telling me to be cool, I probably would have gone off on both of them.

"We bumped into each other, Nek," I said with an eye roll.

"Seems like it was planned to me," she sang as she walked out of the store.

I cut my eyes at her and Cassim pulled my attention away with a light smack on my ass. We connected eyes and my heart skipped a beat. Cass's calloused hands rubbed against the bare skin of my arms, and I shuddered, as goosebumps covered them.

Sometimes, while staring in his eyes, I still lost my voice. Sometimes, the world stood still, like before, and all I could see, smell, and hear was him. Sometimes, the beating of my heart still thumped loudly in my ears.

Sometimes, things went back to the way they were before. To that time where I couldn't move when his hands touched me. Sometimes, was now.

He ran his hand over the side of my face, and I closed my eyes and leaned into it.

"I missed you," I said with my face resting on his hand like we were the only two people in the whole world.

"You just saw me last night," he said with a chuckle.

"So? Yo black ass missed me too," I joked as I moved away from his hand and the rest of the word came alive.

"Let me steal baby away from y'all for a minute," said Cass before tossing the panties he had in his hands into the wrong bin. He grabbed my hand and lead me out of the store. I could hear LeeLee complaining as we walked out of the store. As soon as we did, Cass pinned me up against the wall and kissed me.

I moaned in his mouth as he slipped some tongue inside. He snaked his hand around my body and grabbed a handful of my ass while he tongued me down like the mall wasn't crowded. Like there wasn't a family of three sitting on the benches right behind us. He didn't care, and I didn't give a damn either.

Not while his hands were on me.

Not while his tongue was dancing around my mouth.

Got damn, I done fell in love with the bad guy. And baby, listen… not one fuck was given. This *bad guy* treated me better than any good guy ever could. His thug loving was just what my feisty ass needed. The thug in him kept me in line. Look at him now, gripping my ass, kissing me like he wanted to devour me right now where we stood. And he was angry. Mad because I had acted up and caused a scene. Quiet as kept, Cassim loved that shit. He loved the thug in me just as much as I loved it in him.

"Oh, what's that?" I said as I grabbed his dick through his True Religion shorts.

Cass bit his bottom lip and looked down at my hand gripping his dick, "Stop playing before I have yo lil' bad ass bent over in the handicap stall."

I bit my lip and moved my hand over his hard-on, "Come on."

He closed his eyes and ran that wet thick tongue over his bottom lip before picking me up. I laughed as I wrapped my legs around his waist. He gripped my ass cheeks as he walked me to the bathroom, serious as fuck.

I laughed, "Cass... put me down. I was just playin."

"Uh, uh," he said with half a smile. "You getting this dick."

He boldly pushed the door to the ladies room and walked inside like he belonged in there.

"What the fuck," I heard someone say.

"Shut yo ass up," rudely said Cass.

I buried my face in his neck, cracking the hell up in embarrassment. This nigga truly gave no fucks. He pushed the handicap stall open and finally put me down. I tried to get around him, out of the bathroom but he blocked my path.

"Those laughs gon' be replaced with moans in about," he paused and unbuttoned his shorts. "About five seconds."

"Cassssim," I whined with laughter. "This bathroom is full of bitches."

He grabbed my wrist and pinned them over my head as he kissed and sucked on my neck, "Gon be a bathroom full of mad, jealous bitches in about…" he paused and pulled his boxers down, "Three seconds."

He hiked my sundress up over my ass and picked me up. He ripped my thin thong off and dipped his dick inside of me. I closed my eyes and moaned as soon as I felt it slide in. I didn't give a got damn about the bathroom full of people. They vanished. It was now just Cassim and I, and I treated it as such too. I didn't muffle my moans. I didn't bite into his shoulder. I let my pleasure be heard.

"Fuck," said Cassim into my ear as he penetrated me deeper by spreading my ass cheeks.

I wrapped my arms around his neck and grabbed a handful of his ponytailed dreads. My eyes rolled to the back of my head as he stirred his thick, throbbing dick inside of my wetness. He kissed me on my neck and then softly sucked. The rest of the world continued to fade as I felt an orgasm washing over me.

I moaned like we were in the privacy of our own home.

And Cassim fucked me against the bathroom stall like we weren't in public. In a bathroom full of people.

"Tell me," he grunted as he slammed me up and down over his massive dick.

"It's yours. I'm yours," I yelled as my titties popped out of my top.

He lowly growled as he slammed my back against the stall and slid me up it a bit. Until my pussy was leveled with his mouth. I wrapped my legs around his neck as he twirled his tongue around in my wetness.

"Don't… don't drop me," I moaned as he continued to feast on me.

His only response was holding me tighter and rapidly flicking his tongue over my swollen, pulsating clit.

He sucked on me and made noises with his mouth like my pussy was the best thing he'd ever eaten.

"Ohhhh.. ohhh, Cassss," I purred as I began to shake and tingle.

Without warning, he pulled me down from around his neck, and slid his dick back inside of my creamy pussy. He locked eyes with me as he slowly, and passionately fucked me... in the public restroom of Fairlane Town Center.

"Right there," I said in his ear before biting his shoulder.

"Right there?" he asked before he dug deeper, "Or...or right here."

"Ohhhhh. Everywhere. Just.. fuck me, baby."

He grunted and began to slam me up and down on his dick again. He leaned forward and began to intensely suck on my neck. In between sucking, I heard him mumble a few things that I couldn't make out. Was this nigga speaking in tongues?

His pace slowed up and I knew he was on the verge of cumming. He couldn't cum inside of me. If he did, I would for sure get pregnant again because of how fertile the last pregnancy had me. I tried to wiggle away, but Cassim had a lethal grip on me.

He pulled away from my neck and stared into my eyes, with his lips pulled into his mouth, and a frown of pure ecstasy painted on his face.

His eye contact was heavy. I felt a wave of emotions come over me as I stared back at him. He had that look in his eyes—the one that said 'I found it'. The one that spoke so many unspoken words. I was stuck. He was stuck.

There was no pulling out. And again, I let him cum all inside of me.

*

Two hours later, I was posted up with my girls, sitting on the porch as usual, sipping on something, laughing for a change. I was in a good mood. I was still a little fucked up behind what Goose did to Dinero's family, but life goes on. And dwelling on the past ain't never did me any good.

"Ken always snapping," said Ashlee twerking her ass to Kendrick Lamar's verse on Mask Off remix.

Uh, I got a halo
I level up every time God say so
Shooter on payroll
Lookin' like Pancho, lookin' like Pedro
Money tree from Tarzan
Ten dividends gon' grow when I say "grow"
Kung Fu Kenny with the Midas touch
Ain't no penny that I don't touch
All my enemy bite on dust
Ain't no talkin' when it's fatal
Havin' heart, I can't tell
Half of y'all might need help
I might fall in Rodeo (bitch)
I might ball in Australia (say no more)

Shaneka jumped up from her chair and started twerking her ass against Ashlee's. I sat there waving my hand in the air with a smile on my face.

"Ayyy, Ayyy. Fuck 'eet up," I said all hoodratishly.

"These bitches," said Omni with a laugh as she took a sip of her drink.

The block was popping and all eyes were on the chocolate slim thicks, twerking their asses to that crazy ass Mask Off beat.

LeeLee and Nek loved attention and they were getting just that. They always tried to get me to cut up with them but I'm not even that type. I could get the attention they desired by just sitting back on some mellow shit. I wasn't with the extras, and most of the time I didn't even want attention. If you caught me dancing, acting a fool, my song had to be on, or I was drunk as hell.

"Ay. Ay. Ay," I said pausing after every 'ay' egging these lil' freak bitches on.

Omni fell over onto me, cracking up, "You love getting them started."

I stood up and waved my arms in the air, pointing down at them while they continued to twerk their asses, "Get it cousin. Fuck it up cousinnnnn."

All fun stopped when Juice pulled up in front of the house though. Shaneka stopped bouncing her one ass cheek and LeeLee stopped making her whole ass jiggle as soon as that nigga pulled up at the curb. I even sat down and widened my eyes with a slight giggle as I took another sip of my drink.

Time stood still for a minute, when the passenger door opened, and a bitch hopped out. All of our heads snapped in Omni's direction.

"Om—

She pushed past me and my cousins and stormed down the stairs. Juice hopped out and threw his head back in an 'aw shit' fashion when he noticed Omni. She was supposed to be at work, and he was surprised as hell to see her.

"I thought you had to work, Omni," he yelled as he made his way around the car.

The girl rolled her eyes and turned to walk down the sidewalk in the other direction.

"Surprise! Change of plans, motherfucker," Omni yelled like a crazy woman.

"Fuck you do? Call off so you can post up on the block acting like a hood rat getting drunk and shit."

"Now, nigga you know daaaaamn well Omni ain't a rat," I yelled, putting my little two cents in.

His clown ass was trying to play reverse psychology and Omni wasn't falling for it. She was on his ass. Cursing him out, demanding attention and all of that. But Juice ignored her and climbed the stairs.

"Mind yo own business, Ryann," dismissively said Juice.

"You better be happy she been minding her business," said LeeLee with her lips up to her cup being petty.

Everybody but Omni knew that Juice was cheating on Om. It wasn't a fucking secret around these parts. Well, it was a secret to Omni. She was so busy following behind and demanding answers from Juice that she didn't even catch the smart remark Ashlee had made.

They walked into the house and I shook my head.

"You need to tell her, Ryann. You would want to know if yo nigga was fucking with other bitches behind your back, wouldn't you?" said Shaneka.

I cut my eyes at her, "Of course I would want to know. But then again, I'm not a regular bitch. I would straight leave his ass. Omni? She ain't goin nowhere. Telling her will only cause bad blood between us."

"Right. Nek, shut up."

Since Shaneka and I got into that fight, shit has been mad awkward between us as I expected it to be since I did beat her ass. She and I weren't as cool as we use to be, but since we were cousins it was brushed under the rug. By me it was at least. Nek still had some kind of animosity towards me, but I was quite sure it went back before that fight. She had been acting strange for weeks. I didn't really care too much to find out why, but I knew there was something up.

"Who the fuck is she, Juice? Is she the reason you've been avoiding me," I heard Omni crying in the house.

I rolled my eyes and turned the volume to the sound bar we had sitting on the porch up higher.

What the hell is Omni in there crying for? Like I would've have gone right upside that niggas head. Fuck that. He would have been crying. And I would have sat there and let Omni go to work on him because Juice deserved that shit. Any other female trying to put hands on one of my brothers would get this work. But Omni got a pass for many reasons.

The girl lived a couple of houses down and the ride could have been innocent. I heard him say he picked the bitch up from the bus stop, but I didn't believe it. I didn't put anything past Juices' thotting ass. He's the type of nigga who'll fuck anything with a pussy.

The song switched from Mask Off to DNA, and my cousins went back to twerking like the freak bitches they are. I tilted my cup up to my mouth and giggled, watching them cut up.

Crash!

The loud sound of something breaking, made me jump up from my seat. I pushed past LeeLee and Nek and ran into the house. "What the fuck," I yelled at the sight of my fifty inch TV laid on its face.

"I'll get you another one," said Juice before sitting down on the couch to light a cigarette.

Omni stood in the corner, shaking like a leaf on a tree. I squinted at her and asked, "Omniel, did this nigga just hit you?"

She rapidly shook her head and moved her wild hair out of her face.

I walked over to the couch and pushed Juice upside his head, "Nigga, you hit her?"

He jerked away from me and waved me off, "Gone the fuck on somewhere—

"Did you fuckin' hit her," I screamed at the top of my lungs.

"I'm good Ryann. I told you...He didn't hit me. Mind yo own business, alright," snapped Omni at me.

I squinted at her again and drew back. Before I snapped on her, I sighed and pulled my lips into my mouth. She didn't mean that. She was upset and embarrassed.

I walked away from Juice and stood in front of Omni. I cupped her face in my hands and stared into her beautiful brown eyes. Sadness swam in them, and I felt so bad for my friend. My eyes moved from her eyes, down to her full pink lips, where I discovered a small cut in the corner of her mouth.

"What did he do," I whispered as I watched tears fall from her eyes.

She ran her tongue over the corner of her mouth and looked away, "Nothing. I said I was fine, Ryann."

She snatched her face out of my grips and stormed out of the house. Juice sat there on the couch, looking down at his phone, unbothered by Omni's tears, and my broken TV. My nostrils flared as I marched over to him.

SLAP!

I drew back and slapped him as hard as I could across his face. His head flung in the other direction, and before I could hit him again he had dropped both his burning cigarette and his phone in his lap and grabbed my wrist.

"What the fuck are you doing, Ry?" he yelled as he jumped up from his seat.

"Let her go," calmly said Goose after walking into the house. He stepped over the broken TV, right by us, and went into the kitchen.

Juice let me go and picked his burnt-out cigarette up from the floor.

"What the fuck are you doin, nigga? You hittin on Omni now," I yelled.

Juice roughly scratched at his head, clenching and unclenching his jaw, "Stay out of it, Ryann."

I pointed my finger in his face, "You got it fucked up if you think I'm going to sit back and let you hit on my best friend. Letting you cheat on her was one thing... but this—

"You knew he was cheating on me, Ryann?" said Omni.

I didn't even hear her come back into the house. I turned around to face her and rolled my eyes up, "Yes I knew. And I didn't tell you because I knew you'd do exactly what it is you're doing now—letting the shit ride."

She wiped her nose with the back of her hand and said, "That's not the point, Ryann!"

I was so uninterested in this fucking conversation it made no sense. Hell, she snapped on me for trying to interfere with Juice hitting on her. She would have done the same fuckin' thing if I told her he cheated. Bitches don't be wanting to hear that shit.

"You mad at me because your nigga couldn't keep his dick between the two of you? Omni, be serious."

I was over the dramatics at this point. She was simply deflecting the anger she had towards Juice onto me. I wasn't here for it and Omni knew that. I would snap on her in a second and call her in a few hours like nothing even happened.

That is what best friends do, they fight and get right back to it because life just wouldn't be the same if shit was kept up. But by the look in Omni's eyes, I could tell that this was far from one of our normal little disagreements. She was hurt, but to be honest, I still felt like most of that pain came from the hurt Juice put on her.

"Om—

She put her hand up, "It's okay. I understand. It's a Mosley thing, right? The bond you all have is a lot thicker than the one you're supposed to share with me, right?"

I sighed, "It's not even like that."

But it was. Blood would always be thicker than water. These niggas go crazy hard for me, it's only right that I do the same. I might not agree with what it is that they do, but I support and protect them because it's what they do for me. Juice was wrong, I've already admitted that, but my loyalty lies with him.

"Fuck each and every last one of you Mosley's, aight," said Omni before storming out of the house.

Juice jumped up and followed right behind her. I placed my hands on my hips, looking down at my broken TV. Now ain't that a bitch?

*

"What are you doing, Ryann?" asked Cass, peeking his eyes open.

"Shhh. Don't move," I said as I sat across his chest, with my camera in his face.

After falling out with Omni, I left the house and linked with Cassim. We went out to dinner and straight back to the crib. We watched a movie, fucked, and passed out.

I had to capture this moment. The streetlight from outside of the bedroom window shone on his dark skin with perfection. I didn't care that he was uncomfortable with my camera so close to his face. I didn't care that he didn't like the fact that I was taking pictures of him while he slept. At least I was no longer doing it from a distance without his knowledge.

I bit my bottom lip and slightly moaned as my camera shutter sounded. It had been so long since I photographed him. While I sat up next to him, unable to sleep, I got a glimpse of this perfection. Of my king sleeping peacefully, with his mouth slightly ajar and a subtle furrow in his eyebrows. I wondered; what was he dreaming about? Staring at how the light from outside shined on him was absolutely beautiful. So, I slipped out of bed and grabbed my camera. I'd already taken five, at different angels. But this one? Straight on? Was absolutely breathtaking. His dreads laid messily on his pillow, undone, flowing freely. Just the way I preferred them.

"You done—

"Shhh," I said as I zoomed out a bit and took the final shot. "Done."

"Beth Gallagher ass nigga," said Cass as he pulled me down onto his chest.

"Ups," I said as I lightly thumped him on the lip. "I watched the movie and Beth Gallagher was the wife. Not the stalker—her name was Alex, nigga."

He laughed and held me tighter, "Shit, I knew it was one of them bitches." Cass paused and grabbed his phone from the nightstand. "It's three in the morning. What you doin up with a camera in my face?"

I shrugged and fumbled with one of his locks, "Couldn't sleep."

He kissed the top of my head and rubbed his hand over my ass, "You aight, sweetheart?"

I nestled closer to him, "Mmhm, I am now."

The next morning, I woke up before he did. The sun rise peeking through the swaying drapes woke me up, so I grabbed my camera and climbed out of bed. I slid the drapes open, and stepped out onto the balcony. The view was amazing up here. But I could barely focus on getting a picture of the sunrise because some white bitch way on the other side of the fence was staring at me. I moved the camera away from my face and looked over the balcony at her, "Can I help you with something?"

"Oh… no… good morning," she sweetly said before hurrying out of her backyard.

What the fuck was that about?

Chapter Five . Cass

"Happy birthday to you… Happy birthday to you… Happy birthday to Cassim…Happy birthday to you," sang Ryann as she approached me with a birthday cake illuminated by what looked like exactly twenty-six candles.

I rested back against the cream leather seats with half a smile on my face.

It was after midnight, and technically my birthday. Shorty had gone above and beyond to make this night special for me. She'd chartered a Yacht, on some laid back, just she and I type of shit, and all that. It felt good to be appreciated. It felt good for it to really be genuine this time. Baby didn't care about the money or my hood status. All she cared about was me—she was obsessed with a nigga and I low key loved it.

I hated my birthday, but I didn't tell her that. I let her do her thing. And when she came at me with the surprises, I was legit…surprised. Ryann took time and consideration when she planned this. She did not know I hated my birthday, but she did know that I wasn't the club type of nigga. Even knowing that, she could have had this bitch flooded with my niggas. But she knew that nine times out of ten, I didn't want to see them cats. She knew the small things about me because she paid attention to detail. She was of a rare breed. I say that a lot because it's true. Anybody else would have thrown me a huge party at one of the most popping clubs in the D. And you know why? Because of my hood status. Because they knew that one mention of my name would bring the whole city out. But Ryann…she didn't care about shit like that

She sat the cake on the table in front of me, before leaning over and kissing me on the lips, "Happy birthday, baby."

I gripped a handful of her ass through the sheer cover-up she wore and said, "Thank you, sweetheart."

She blushed and stepped back with her hands on her hips, "Make a wish."

I looked down at the plethora of candles in a slight daze. There was a time in my life when I didn't even know my birthday. I didn't learn it until I stayed with my first foster parents. When I thought that maybe somebody could love my black ass. It was with them that I had my very first birthday party. Shit was live. All of the foster kids and the kids in the neighborhood showed mad love.

When shit was flipped, and I was sent to stay with Anna and Tyrone, my birthday was celebrated in other ways. Ways that made me hate the day I was born.

I looked away from the cake and up at her before standing up. She looked up at me with a smile, and a twinkle in her eye that I knew that only I could put there and said, "What? What's wrong?"

I ran my hands over her smooth arms before grabbing hold of them, "Nothing, sweetheart. For the first time in my life... everything is right."

She blushed and looked away, "Are you going to make a wish, Cassim?"

I kept my eyes on her. She kept blushing away... shit like that drove me crazy. Baby was so into me that sometimes I had to remind her crazy ass to breath. It was shit like that, that told me that I had the right one. It took us a minute to get where we are now, but I'm happy I did decide to stick it out.

"I don't have anything to wish for. I've got everything I need, sweetheart," I said as I ran my hand over her cheek which she leaned into with closed eyes.

"Cassim," she purred.

Where did this woman come from? She was perfection.

When I was a kid, I longed for shit like this, but as I grew up, I stopped giving a fuck. I stopped looking for love and just embraced the savage in me. She was exactly what I needed though. She took care of me in ways I thought I didn't need to be taken care of in.

Ryann not only told me she loved me—she showed it too. I've had women claim to be in love with me. And I've had women try to prove it to me too. But it wasn't this. Nothing had ever been like this. A yacht? A cake? Singing happy birthday to me? Shits genuine.

"You know... you're fuckin' perfect, right?" I seriously said.

She opened her eyes and blinked a few times before saying, "No, I'm not."

"Yes. You are."

She cleared her throat and backed away, "Come on... blow the candles out before they burn out, Cass."

She didn't like for me to call her perfect, and I didn't like it when she said I had a perfect face. What I said was the truth though, so why she shied away from factual shit was a wonder to me.

I sighed and blew the candles out. No wish. No thought. Nothing. Just blew them out to please her. I would do anything to please her ass. My dedication to her went deeper than just some fuckin' candles. My dedication to Ryann was brought on by her dedication to me. I've never been dedicated to a fuckin' thing in my life. But for her... for her I would move mountains. Or shit... at least try to.

I leaned forward and scooped up some of the icing of the cake with my mouth just to annoy her germaphobe ass.

She sucked her teeth, "Ugggggh Cassim. Why'd you just do that? You couldn't use a fork? I don't even want anymore."

I smirked and pulled her closed to me by grabbing her by the waist, "Why not? Shorty... my germs don't mean shit when my DNA been swimming all up and around them tonsils."

She cracked up laughing and playfully hit me in the chest, "Shut up nigga."

I sat her on my lap, grabbed her by the chin, and kissed her.. dipped my icing coated tongue all up in her sweet ass mouth. She wrapped her arms around my neck and moaned in my mouth.

I pulled away from the kiss and placed both my hands on the sides of her face, "Thank you, sweetheart."

She smiled, and that twinkle in her eye shined brighter than the stars in the sky, "You deserve it."

"You think that, huh?" I asked before licking my lips.

Her eyebrows knitted together in confusion, "Of course you do. You mean the world to me."

"That's it," I sucked my teeth. "Shit baby... you half steppin... you *are* the world to me."

She blushed.

That fuckin' blushing that got me where I'm at today. Stuck on her, on some cake type of shit.

*

"Pass me the L, pussy," I said as I sat slouched down in Luck's whip.

Wavy scooted to the edge of the backseat and passed me the blunt. I grabbed it from in between his fingers and took three pulls from it before passing it back and pulling my Detroit fitted lower over my eyes.

Play time with the queen was over. The short time away with baby was therapeutic in more ways than one. I almost forgot about this empire I'm trying to build. Being with baby took all of the worries of the outside away. But we had to get back. She had the photography thing going on, and I had this drug shit going on.

I was riding with Luck and Wavy. We were on a mission. A money mission, but unfortunately that money mission was at a club. I was linking with the club owner about getting some of my shit floating around that bitch. Mandees was a bar and grill but that bitch slapped heavy like it was a club. The club scene ain't never been my favorite, but if it was about cheese, I was on it.

"Sinn gon' make me fuck her up," said Luck.

I sat up and pulled my buffs off my face. Crossing the parking lot right in front of Luck's old school Monte was his Baby Moms', Sinn, and her sister, Symphony, laughing with four other girls.

"Ah shit," I said with a sigh.

The last person I ever wanted to see was Symphony.

"She ain't gone start shit with you, bruh," said Luck as he eased into a parking space.

Symphony never went to the club sober. Bitch was definitely lifted and would most likely pop off recklessly on some ol' reminiscence, emotional shit. The type of drama a nigga never wanted. I hated seeing the bitch. If she wasn't mugging me all crazy like, she was throwing subs, talking in circles and all that.

"Let's get this shit over with," I said as I took a swig of water from my Aquafina bottle.

Luck killed the engine, and the three of us got out of the whip. The parking lot, and was flooded with thot bitches, and niggas stunting hard for 'em. That's Detroit niggas for you though. They love the attention I hate. All these bums out here with their sounds on bang, blasting Kendrick Lamar's DNA, yelling at the thotties and these bitches steady grillin me. In my face, smiling, throwing the pussy at me without verbalizing it.

"Shit baby thick," said Wavy, animatedly forming an O with his lips. "She on you, G."

I pinched the tip of my nose and made my way through the crowds, ignoring the lingering hands of bum niggas I didn't know who tried to show love. Love I didn't want. Shit I didn't need.

We made our way in the bar and Luck wrapped his arms around Sinn's waist from the back. She turned around, ready to smack the hell out of bro. But when she turned around and seen who it was, she smiled and wrapped her arms around his neck.

"Hey daddy," she said before kissing him.

I took my glasses off and looked around the bar for the owner.

"Hey stranger, you can't speak?" said Symphony with a hint of sarcasm in her voice.

"What up doe," I nonchalantly replied.

"Hey Cass. You alright tonight," asked Sinn with a sweet smile.

"Shit yeah, I'm smooth sis," I tapped Luck on the arm. "Money mission, bruh."

I didn't give a fuck about him feeling territorial over his chick. Sinn's a gorgeous ass, chubby girl with enough confidence to rock a cut off top, and skin tight jeans. Shorty had an aura about her and Luck was worried about a goofy pushing up on her. I got it. But if Ryann was around here, I would still be on the same mission I was on before I saw her ass.

"Shit baby, what's good with you," said Wavy to Symphony who sucked her teeth and stood next to me. "You've been alright, Cassim?"

I looked down at her, calling me by my real name and the corner of my top lip curled up into a frown, "Stop playin with me, Symphony."

She giggled and playfully hit me on the arm, "Why you so mad? It's a beautiful night."

I walked away from her and headed straight to the bar with Luck and Wavy walking behind me.

Symphony did that type of shit on purpose. She knew off back that I didn't like to be called Cassim in person. Goofy type bitch was trying to name drop in front of Wavy like the nigga didn't already know my real name. Clown.

"Shit boss, I'm trying to get on some of these hos. Once we wrap—

"Go," I told Wavy cutting him off. "Party, G."

I didn't need him here and didn't know why he was here to begin with. Wavy annoyed the whole fuck out a nigga. When it came to these bitches, I wasn't moved by 'em. The only lady my dick could get hard for these days was Ryann. She did it for me on all levels. Nothing out here compared to her. So, walking around the bar, I had tunnel vision. I didn't see shit but the money I was going to make by flooding my shit in this bitch.

Wavy said, "You sho'—

"Walk off, Wav," said Luck dismissively.

Wavy nodded and walked away.

I stood at the bar and called the bartender down with a head nod. She smiled and sashayed down to my end of the bar.

"Hey Cass. What can I get for you, handsome?"

"Freddie."

She nodded, and smiled at Luck before walking off. Luck was busy watching every move Sinn made. I tapped him on the arm to grab his attention from his shorty.

"Yo," he said with raised eyebrows.

"You smooth, G," I asked with a slight chuckle as I leaned my back against the bar.

Luck shook his head with a smile and blew out a gust of air, "G... Niggas liable to catch a body out here. Na' talm bout?"

"Nah, dawg I don't," I seriously told him. I tapped at my temple, "Use ya head, bro."

"I will... as much as possible."

"Niggas know you posted. Shits gonna be straight."

Luck was crazy when it came to Sinn. They've been rocking for years. She was with him from the bottom, and he would literally catch a body if a nigga came at her sideways while he was present. I knew this because I've witnessed it happen.

"Cass... Luck... what's good," said Freddie with his hand extended.

I looked down at, briefly before slapping hands with him. Right after, Luck slapped hands with him, but his eyes stayed on Sinn and her girls on the dancefloor.

The three of us walked off, heading towards Freddie's office.

When we got to the office, Freddie tried to create small talk, but I let him know that I wasn't here for the chitchat.

"Fuck all that, G," I said as I put my hands behind my head. "Let's rap about this paper."

Freddie chuckled, and glanced at Luck, while he leaned back on his chair, "Not friendly today, huh, my mans?"

"Friendly?" I asked with a chuckle before lightly hitting Luck in the arm, "When have I ever been friendly, bruh?"

"Freddie prolly got you mixed up," said Luck staring Freddie in the eyes.

"Shit yeah," I said before interlocking my fingers behind my head. "Sound about right."

Luck and I were fuckin' with Freddie and it was clearly getting to him. It took Luck to crack a smile for him to loosen up.

"Y'all niggas," he said with a light laugh.

I smirked, "Let's get down to the bread though."

I unlocked my fingers and sat up, ready to talk numbers.

*

"Where you running off to? The night is still young," said Symphony, jogging up behind me as I headed out of the bar.

I glanced over my shoulder at her and kept walking. I didn't know what the fuck shorty was on, but I wasn't with it. She was dead ass following me out of the club like we were cordial or some shit like that.

"Cass—

"What's good, Symphony? What chu following me for, darlin?" I asked as I leaned up against Luck's car.

She narrowed her eyes at me and pointed, "Un un, don't you dare call me darlin'. I know what that shit really means."

She was trying to be nice and I couldn't put a finger on why. Bitches like Symphony were only nice when they wanted something. Low key, she didn't have a nice bone in her body. Not towards me. Not since I broke her heart.

"What do you want, Symphony?" I asked her with the corners of my mouth slightly turned up.

"Why do I have to want something to talk to a friend?" she asked as she leaned up against Luck's whip next to me.

"Friend? You frontin' heavy. I don't know what ya motive is, but miss me with it, aight," I said with a huff.

Before she could say anything else, Sinn and Luck walked up.

"NeeNee," yelled Sinn laughing, holding onto Luck's arm. "Leave Cass alone, wit yo damn near married ass. He gotta girlfriend now, he ain't thinkin about you."

Symphony sucked her teeth, and looked me up and down, "This nigga don't care about a title. Ain't that right?"

"Fuck up outta here, shorty," I said as I tore into a pack of Winterfresh gum, "Luck, you ready, G?"

"Why you acting like a bitter ex, Symphony?" asked Sinn standing in front of her sister with her hands on her hips.

"Bitter for what? Todd is ten times more of a man than he could ever dream of being."

I snorted, "If that was true you wouldn't have had to say it, darlin. Boastin' ass," I pushed away from the car and grabbed the door handle, "Come on Luck, lets skate."

"I said it because—

"Did I give you the impression that I cared, my baby? Aw shit, my fault," I said interrupting her.

Sinn playfully hit me in the arm and said, "Stop Cass. Listen," she leaned into the car, "I was thinking... I know you kind of antisocial and all 'lat... but I think it'd be fun to go to Atlantic City or Miami or something together. The four of us. Ask your girl... see if she'll be cool with that."

"Aight."

She smiled and went back to conversing with her mad ass sister.

A few seconds later, Luck hopped in and cranked the engine up. I asked him where Wavy was and he said the nigga was staying.

He burnt off, and glanced at me with a smirk.

"Fucks that about, nigga," I asked as I started to bust a Backwood down.

"Sis on you," he goofily said.

"Nah she want something."

"Meat," he replied.

We chuckled and I shook my head. What bruh was talkin' about could very well be legit but on the other hand, Symphony wasn't really trying to fuck with me like that. She wanted something, but I didn't think it was dick.

*

I slid into bed and wrapped my arms around her body. She purred and pressed up against me. I ran my hands down her body, ready to grip bare ass cheeks but they were covered in panties. Big granny type panties too.

"Fuck is this," I said as I popped the elastic band.

"Ummmm. Panties," she replied.

"You know fuck well I don't allow panties in my bed," I joked as I began to lower them.

She giggled and smacked my hand away, "Issa period, nigga."

Anybody else would have dead ass been out of the door. But when I was with Ryann, it was more than just sex. Baby stimulated my mind.

"That mouth still work though, don't it?" I joked.

She turned around and playfully hit me in the chest, "Yo ol' disrespectful ass."

I held my hands up, "My bad—

She shut me up, when I felt her hands gripping the base of my dick, "If you wash this sweaty fucker, I'll suck the skin off."

My eyebrows shot up, "Shit sweetheart. I need the skin but let me go get this mafucka squeaky for you."

She cracked up laughing while I hopped out the bed for a quick shower.

*

The next morning, I woke up to the smell of breakfast. A nigga dead ass laid there, savoring the smell of my kitchen finally being used. I swear, I don't think the skillet has ever been used. I didn't even know where Ryann got food from because the 'fridge was on E.

I reached over to my nightstand and grabbed my phone. I had a few text messages and a couple of missed calls, that I ignored. Shit, a nigga was trying to eat. I hope baby knew how to cook.

I sat up and rubbed my eyes before slipping my feet into my Nike slides. On my way down the stairs to the kitchen, I could hear pots and pans knocking, and music playing at a subtle level.

Ryann moved around the kitchen singing, "Roll with it all you gotta do is roll with it.. Let me into your system baby yeah, roll with it... Said I got what you missing...You ain't gotta go get it when I pull up with that work for you baby come get it..."

I crept behind her and wrapped my arms around her. She flinched, and greeted me with a kiss, "Good morning."

"Morning, what you got for a nigga," I asked as I slipped my arms from around her to take in all of the food sitting on the kitchen island.

"Blueberry pancakes, sausage links, eggs, grits and hash browns," she said as she turned back around to the stove. "After that nut you bust last night, I know you about hungry as fuck."

I laughed and smacked her on the ass, "Good looks on the fire ass dome, my baby."

Ryann was a totally different chick from when I first approached her. She still had that mean streak, but baby goofy as fuck.

I sat at the kitchen island and said, "I can get use to this. Going to sleep to head, waking up to breakfast."

She looked over her shoulder at me and said, "What you trying to say?"

"What I've been saying," I said as I grabbed a sausage link from the tray.

I been wanted Ryann to move on. I didn't like the neighborhood she was resting in. True enough her brothers were some respected niggas but it wasn't a secret that they were treacherous. And although not many people knew about the princess, a lot of people in the hood did and mafuckas simply cannot be trusted.

"Let me talk to Juice first," she said as she turned the burners off.

"For what," I asked before biting into my sausage.

She shrugged and began to fix my plate, "You know how my brothers are."

"They already know what's what."

Them niggas respected me. The respect was mutual between her brothers and I.

"Even if they do, I still have to run it by them, babe," she said as she poured me some orange juice.

"Understood."

She sat across from me and started to dig into her plate, but for some reason, I grabbed her hand and told her to bow her head.

She looked up at me with furrowed eyebrows but she bowed her head anyway. I thanked God for the food and said amen.

"Shortest grace I've ever heard," said Ryann with a laugh as she poured syrup on her pancakes.

"Don't matter—I gave thanks. You was about to stuff ya face without saying anything," I joked.

She rolled her eyes, "Whatever."

I smirked and cut my pancakes in squares, "Yo, what's good? You got some gigs lined up? Or you trying to go on a lil' trip?"

Her eyes widened, "A trip? Where?"

"Atlantic City."

"Let's goooo," she dramatically replied. "I cannot wait. How we getting there?" She smiled mischievously, "You should charter a jet. I know I'll get a crazy thrill out of sucking the soul out of yo dick—

I cracked up laughing, "Man, what? Shorty, you wild." I laughed some more before saying, "Listen, Luck and his girl Sinn invited us. Ain't gon be no suckin' the soul out of this mafucka on the jet. We can fa sho save that for next time, though."

She drew back, "His girl? Is she cool? You know I don't really do new bitches."

I scooped up a forkful of pancakes, dripping in syrup, "She straight. Real spit. Sinn's mad cool. I think y'all will get along just fine."

Sinn was sis. She was the realist, trillest broad my nigga Luck fucked with. She's held bro down on several occasions. She was hood and a real ass thoroughbred. She and Ryann had a lot in common, so I knew shorty would end up liking her.

Ryann picked up a piece of bacon and bit into it before saying, "Alright now. I don't want to end up beating Luck's bitch up."

MISS CANDICE

Chapter Six . Ryann

"Where you about to go?" asked Nek, standing in my doorway while I packed for the trip to Atlantic City. I was ready for a change of scenery. Being around this bitch all day every day was whack.

"AC," I replied.

"That's wassup. For how long?"

"Just the night."

"Aw, yo *hubby* taking you," she said adding emphasis on hubby. "I wish I had me somebody like him. He's the realest."

I frowned a little, "Yeah, that he is. What's up Nek? You wanted something?"

I was bothered. You know how I am about my nigga and the way Nek was standing there gazing with a smile on her face talking about how he was the realest just didn't sit well with me. I felt like I would probably end up smacking her ass at any given moment.

"Naw. I just miss you, that's all. It just seems like since that fight, things been off between us," she said with her bottom lip poked out.

"Things were off between us way before the fight, Nek," I said as I folded a shirt to put in my Gucci luggage.

"Things were different when I got out of the hospital. That's all."

"Like?"

"You and Cass.... You and Dinero—"

"That's my life. What's that gotta do with our relationship, Shaneka?"

I sensed a little jealously in her voice and was basically over the whole conversation.

"It don't," she said with an attitude. "I just saw you making bad decisions and... I just don't think what happened would have happened if—"

"Watch yaself bitch," I said as I pointed my finger at her. "You remember what happened the last time you got besides yo self with the talking, Nek."

She sighed, and licked her lips before saying, "You know what? Never mind, just... enjoy your vacation."

*

"Hey girl, I'm Sinn," said Luck's girlfriend with her hand extended for me to shake.

I stood there, kind of shocked for a minute. Sinn wasn't what you'd expect a nigga like Luck to be with. He was the epitome of a Detroit hood nigga. He wore buffs on the regular, true religion, and all that. Aside from his thugness, that nigga was fine. I can say that without being disrespectful to my man. Luck is tall, with a thick goatee, caramel colored... to be honest, he looked like a ho. Like he had all the bitches lined up ready to suck his dick. So, for him to be with a fluffy chick... it kind of took me by surprise.

I shook her hand, "Ryann."

She smiled, "I know. I've heard all about you."

"I hope all good things," I replied with a phony smile.

I didn't know this bitch from a can of paint and I knew Cass wasn't who she heard things about me from. He didn't do that. He barely talks. So, for her to say she heard a lot about me? Nah.. couldn't have been from my nigga. Probably from a gang of hating bitches because I had this nigga on lock.

"Of course. Luck speaks highly of you," she said. "Sometimes I be having to check that nigga like damn, mafucka is she Cass's bitch or yours?"

I could tell that she was one of those silly broads, so I let that bitch word slide with a little giggle.

We had just boarded the private jet and were on our way to Atlantic City. I needed this trip. After the crazy couple of weeks I'd had, I needed some time to just kick back and enjoy life.

"So, how did y'all meet?" asked Sinn with a sweet smile on her face.

She seemed like a genuinely cool bitch, so I piped down a little bit. We sat on the jet talking most of the trip to Atlantic City, getting to know each other.

*

The Borgata Hotel Casino and Spa was absolutely gorgeous. I had never stayed in anything as lavish as the Vista Room at The Water Club they had there. Shit was straight up presidential—only fit for a King and Queen. It was bigger than my whole fucking house. Cassim had to spend some serious bread to stay here.

"This is so nice," I complimented as I slid my shoes off.

"It's aight," Cassim jokingly said. "What's good? You ready to go cut up on the crap table?"

"I'm a slots type of gal," I said as I let my hair down. "First, I want to shower."

I was kind of pissed that I was on my period. The shower was lit as fuck. I wanted to throw my ass all over his dick under the waterfall shower. It's aight, I'm making sure we come back here. It's a must. And next time, we will be alone. Not doing this ol' couple type of mess. I just wanted some alone time with my bae. I didn't care that all of the time we spent together was alone either. I preferred it that way.

Aside from wanting to be selfish, though, I kind of enjoyed Sinn and Luck's company. They were so different from Cassim and I. Cass and I are always touchy feely, whereas Sinn and Luck are more so laid back and not so affectionate. Sinn said that what Cassim and I are on is the cutesy, lovey-dovey stage. Bold bitch had the audacity to say that in a couple of years, I would end up hating the sight of him.

Never.

I could never hate the sight of him. I didn't know Sinn and Luck's history, but I did know that they've been together since they were teenagers and 'they don' been through some shit' as she put it. I didn't ask for her to go into detail. For one, I just met the bitch. Two, I didn't care enough to pry. Most likely he cheated, she took him back, and he kept doing it. Typical ain't-shit- nigga type of mess.

*

After my shower, the four of us went down to the casino together. Cassim and Luck slow rolled behind Sinn and I, most likely talking business. Sinn was doing most of the talking. She was eager to get to know me, but I was a little reserved with my business. I've always been like that. I've never been that friendly ass female who told all of her business. Sinn was that type. But she was cool with it though. Most of what she talked about was about she and Luck's kid, Nate. If it wasn't about Nate, she was talking about her hair line, and her cosmetic line to follow. She was business savvy and I liked that about her.

She leaned into me, "Don't put all of your trust in that nigga. Save you some money, girl. Get you a safety net. So, when he act up, and it's time for you to leave, you will be straight."

I laughed and shook my head, "You can't school me baby. I'm hip. I've got three brothers. I'm good, my baby. Trust."

Sinn knew I was new to the lifestyle of being with a dope boy, but what she didn't know was that I was not a good girl. I wasn't timid and shy. I wasn't a push over. If need be, I was a fuckin' savage. Probably more of a savage than her ass.

*

After a night of gambling and a morning of basking in all of the beauty the that The Borgata Hotel Casino and Spa had to offer, it was time to go. I could say that the plane ride back to Michigan was bittersweet. But nothing about the shit was sweet. It was all bitter baby. I hated the sight of the hood. I couldn't wait to move in with Cassim.

I was shocked when he asked me to move in, although I did try to play it off. I was happy he'd asked me because for so long, I've wanted to ask him. He hinted at it a few times, but never came out and blatantly asked me to move in. That's what I was waiting for.

"How was your trip?" sang Nek when I walked through the door.

"Girl, I had a blast," I replied with a smile.

"How much did you win?" asked LeeLee, sitting on the couch next to Nek with her legs pulled underneath her butt, swiping around on her tablet.

"About three hundred," I gloated with a stretch. "Have my brothers been here today?"

"That's what's up," said LeeLee. "Naw. Not yet."

"I thought I heard Juice over here this morning," asked Nek with dipped eyebrows.

Ashlee glanced up at Shaneka and shook her head, "Girl, that was Loc."

"You still fuckin' that nigga in my crib," I asked with a chuckle as I headed to the kitchen for something to drink. "You know what? Have fun, bitch. Have fun! I'm moving out. It's gonna be a process since I've accumulated so much shit over the years. But I'm leaving. you ho's can have an orgy for all I care."

"Aw, really," said Shaneka with a grin on her face. "I'm so happy for you Ryann. Seriously."

I didn't know if she was being genuine or not. I didn't care either way to be honest. I was in too much of a great mood to throw shade or give her the side eye. I simply smiled and thanked her.

Ashlee sighed and said, "Well... we gotta have some celebratory drinks or suh'in."

Shaneka smirked with raised eyebrows, "Drink on Ry?"

"Hell naw. Drinks on you bitches," I joked. "I'm about to toss this up."

I had been trying to save money. I wanted to take my photography to the next level. I wanted a studio. I wanted to hire a team of photographers... I wanted an assistant and all that fancy top notch shit. The clientele had been rolling in, but they've been going unanswered and rescheduled because of the stress I had been under. I could have sent one of my workers to handle those gigs I couldn't handle, you know? It was time to take my craft to the next level.

"Aight, what we sipping on? Extra smooth vodka? Or the 102 proof," joked Ashlee.

"Shit no. Bitch I ain't drinking that poison."

We laughed and I put my things away.

*

We were up to our usual shenanigans. Posted up on the porch, drinking Patron Margaritas. The only thing missing was Omni. I missed her, but I'd be damned if I called or text her. She spazzed out on me. She should be apologizing to me. I know it might seem childish, but I don't care.

"I know y'all heard what happened, right?" said Tiny, walking up the block with her squad.

I looked up from my phone with a frown, "Ashlee, she must be talking to you."

"Nah, I'm really just talking to you," said Tiny with too much base in her voice for my liking "Peewee is going to foster care because of what yo nigga did."

I licked my bottom lip and stuffed my phone in my purse, "My nigga did absolutely nothing, bitch. Carry on."

She didn't though. She actually came closer to the porch with her fist balled like she wanted to throw hands. I sat my phone down and stood up, "What's good, Tiny? You really wanna go there with me?"

Shaneka stood up and put her hands up, "Tiny, Cass ain't do that shit. Why do you care anyway?"

"That's a whole ass lie," she yelled with misty eyes. "That nigga nearly knocked me down the stairs to get into their house, checking them about Dinero. Speaking of D, the nigga probably killed him too. Her nigga!"

I snorted and licked my lips, "Bitch you need to watch what comes out of that raggedy ass mouth of yours. Keep speaking lies and watch me yank you up and toss you down the block."

"Tiny, just fuckin go," said Ashlee. "You bitches really don't want these problems."

It had been years since my cousins and I had to beat up on a group of dusty bitches. I felt like I was getting too old to be out here scrapping, but I would gladly scrub the pavement with Tiny's face.

Tiny smirked and backed away from the porch, "It's cool. Just watch, ho."

I waved her off and sat back down to enjoy the rest of my margarita before I had to start packing.

Chapter Seven . Cass

"I knew something was off about that nigga," said Nino as he bounced a ball, shaking his head from side to side. "The looks he gave Mitch when he kept talm'bout there was a snake in our camp was vicious. Look wasn't of appreciation. Straight murder was in his eyes. Week later, Mitch end up with a bad batch."

I was on the block, checking on shit, and as usual niggas were talking about Chicago. I was dead ass tired of hearing about the nigga. Fuck... can't the dead rest in peace? Or hell... wherever the bitch nigga ended up at.

"Daaaamn, so you sayin," said another young cat rubbing at his chin. "You sayin Chicago gave Mitch that bad batch cause he was on him?"

"Duh, you stupid ass nigga," said Nino with a chuckle. "Peep. Boss... that runner lurkin. Bitch hot about you not giving her dick."

I glanced across the street and sure as shit, Ryann's cousin was sitting on the porch mean mugging me. When she noticed me looking, she smiled and waved. I frowned and turned my attention back to the slice of liquor store pizza I was smashing.

"Shouldn't you niggas be doing something that makes sense? Like... outchea beating the block tryin' get cha coins up. You young niggas stay posted on bullshit like y'all don't have a quota to meet," I said with a mouthful of pizza.

"Ugh.. why is he over here? Shouldn't he be locked up. Fuckin' murderer. Who kills an entire family though?" I heard someone from behind say.

I looked over my shoulder and that rat bitch Tiny was standing there with her face screwed up, and a couple of her girls.

"Yo, can I help you with somethin' darlin?" I asked as I finished my pizza off.

"Yeah, kill yo self! Do the world a favor and take that gun off yo waistband, put that bitch to yo head, and off yoself."

I laughed and balled the greasy aluminum foil the pizza once sat on up and tossed it in the city dumpster sitting on the street. I thought it was funny that just a month or so ago, this same bitch was swallowing a shit load of my kids.

I wiped my hands on the front of my black shirt and reached for the pistol sitting on my waistband. I handed it to her, "Do the world that favor you talm'bout and get rid of me yaself."

She looked back and forth from me and the gun with wide eyes like I was crazy. Luck walked up to me and whispered in my ear, "Nigga is you crazy?"

I moved away from him and treaded towards her. But she kept walking back. I cocked the hammer back and extended the gun out for her to grab, but she kept looking at me with those bucked eyes like I was out of my mind.

"Here. Now all you gotta do is pull the trigger, my baby," I said, steady approaching her.

"Cass," yelled Ryann from across the street.

I glanced over at her, "Good morning, sweetheart. I pray to God that the last pair of shoes I have to see on you are not those fuck ass Fenty slides. Go change 'em."

"Get... get that gun away from me," said Tiny, now forced to stay put because she had backed up against a parked car.

Ryann ran up on me and quickly snatched the gun from me. Within seconds, she broke it down and had hit me upside of the head, "What in the entire fuck is wrong with you, Cass?!"

I looked at her in awe, "Shit baby, let me see that again. And you was talm'bout you didn't care about learning how to bus' a gun down—

"I'm not playing, Cass," she said with a frown on her face. She sideways pointed at Tiny, "Fucks going on here?"

Tiny sucked her teeth and walked away, "Don't nobody want this nigga. Been there done that. I just want him to eat a bullet."

I threw my head back when Ryann's eyeballs nearly popped out of their sockets. "Been there, done that!?"

"Yes bitch. What? You thought you were the only one around here hopping on that dick," Tiny said over her shoulder.

Ryann cocked her head to the side and said, "You fucked that dirty ass hood rat bitch?"

"Just like ya old nigga did," said Tiny running her mouth like Ryann wasn't crazy. "Yo niggas must have a thing for dusty ass hoodrat bitches, huh?"

Ryann's face turned beet red as her nostrils flared, with balled fist, "Cass!"

I grabbed her arms, "Before you. When you were still tied up with that fuck nigga you called a boyfriend. Corn ball ass Uber Driver—

Ryann snatched away from me and looked at me with eyes so cold that if looks could kill, I'd fasho be dead, "You don't think you should have told me that shit, Cass!?"

I grabbed the broken down gun from her and quickly put it back together before stuffing it back inside of my waistband, "You want me to run down a list of the bitches I fucked before you too, sweetheart? Relax; put a smile on that beautiful ass face."

The niggas behind me did nothing but make the situation worst when they laughed at what was going on. I looked over my shoulder at them and told them to go find some business. As expected, the nickel and dime ass niggas pushed off. Wavy and Luck stood against Luck's whip passing a blunt back and forth.

"It was good too bitch—so fuckin' good," said Tiny, now walking backwards down the block with a smile on her face.

Ryann cocked her head to the side and pushed me, "Got me out here looking dumb as fuck!"

Before I could say anything else, she took off running towards Tiny. Before Tiny could prepare for Ryann coming at her, Ryann had already punched her in the face. The whole block went wild, running up the block with their phones out, ready to post shit on social media.

I scratched my cheek and treaded towards the altercation. There was a small crowd forming around them, but when niggas saw me coming, they got out of the way. Ryann was on top of Tiny, doing shorty dirty. I scooped her up and carried her away from the fight on my shoulder.

*

"I can't believe you stuck dick to that nasty, trif ass bitch," said Ryann, standing at my bathroom sink, cleaning her wounded knuckles.

I stood there, resting against the doorframe listening to her go off, without uttering a single word. She was heated. But I believed she was more upset about something else.

"You mad 'cause the Uber driver was smashin' shorty?" I asked, cutting her off midsentence.

Ryann gave me a quick glance over her shoulder before going back to what she was doing, "What?"

I pushed myself up off the doorframe and stood behind her in the mirror. I locked eyes with her reflection and repeated my question.

Her nostrils flared and she rolled her eyes, "Why would I give a fuck? Dinero raped me. He is dead. I don't care—

"But you did care about the nigga. Shit happened before he decided to stupidly—before he did what he did," I said before clearing my throat. "You give a fuck, sweetheart. It's aight."

I couldn't imagine her really being mad about me fucking Tiny. Shit made absolutely no sense for her to be pissed about that. It happened before this happened. So, while I sat back letting her vent, I realized what it really was. Baby went ape shit because Tiny fucked her old dude.

"I said I don't—

"What you trying to eat on tonight, sweetheart?" I asked, deading the subject.

I didn't like to be lied to and Ryann was doing a lot of that. I couldn't understand why when I truly didn't give a shit about her being mad about that. It's a normal reaction. Shorty just found out her dude was cheating on her. She's probably flip fa sho if she knew girl-girl was pregnant.

She looked over her shoulder at me, "Why did you give her your gun? What the fuck was that about? That bird bitch got some serious ass animosity in her heart for you and you give her your gun? What happened to you trying? That shit was straight up reckless."

I sighed and leaned against the back wall, "Baby you gone have to chill with that shit."

Ryann needed to understand that shit like death was beyond my control. True enough, I was on some reckless shit earlier. I didn't give a fuck. Ryann wanted me to. But how was I supposed to change the way I felt about living or dying just to appease her?

"Your fear of death is unrealistic, love," I told her in all honesty. I held her from behind and kissed on her neck as I spoke. "Nothing lasts forever, Ryann."

She jerked away from me and cocked her head to the side so that she would have a better look at me, "You don't think I know that?"

"You don't act like you do."

"I just... I just don't want to think about it, and I don't need you out here handing bitches that hate you guns to fuckin murk you with. That's all. Respect the fact that I do not want to lose you right now," she yelled with tears swimming in her eyes.

She looked away from my reflection and rolled her eyes, "Please. Just do that for me, Cassim."

"Aight, aight," I held her tighter. "You better not let a tear fall, sweetheart. Don't pain a nigga like that."

I hated to upset her. I hated when her overwhelming fear of losing me made her emotional. I always wanted Ryann to smile—she was her most beautiful with a huge grin on her face. To see her cry because I was a knucklehead ass nigga pained me.

I turned her around and kissed her on top of the head, "You want me to change something about myself that's been a part of me for as long as I could remember. It's hard, Ryann."

"You're no longer living for just yourself, Cassim. You have me to live for too."

I was living for no one. Not even myself. I was just existing. But now, I was living for someone. I had to take that into consideration.

Chapter Eight . Ryann

"Aw that's cute, girl," said Sinn, Luck's baby momma, complimenting the bad ass two-piece swimsuit I was rocking.

Usually, I don't do new friends. But since the trip to Atlantic City, Sinn and I had been kind of kicking it. She was a little extra at times, but she was cool as hell and it was kind of nice to hang around someone other than my cousins or Omniel.

Speaking of Omni, I haven't seen her. She really was mad at me for not telling her about Juice cheating on her. I got it. I understood but the kind of chick she is, she would have stayed with that nigga and he would have been pissed with me. On top of that, Omni would have definitely been in my ear all the fucking time questioning me about shit I had no interest in. It was not my responsibility to tell her he was cheating, shit.

I gave her a little smile as I adjusted my booty cheeks, "Thanks Sinn. Your suit is cute too."

Sinn is a cute caramel complexed plus size chick, but she wore her weight with confidence. She was mainly thighs and ass, but she had a gut on her. She was rocking a two-piece bathing suit just like my ass, and she wore it fabulously, okay!?

"Luck is going to blow a fucking gasket when he sees me come outside in this shit," she said with a smirk as she admired her ass.

I laughed and grabbed my towel as I followed her out of the den, which sat right off the back patio of she and Luck's house. They were set up pretty nice in a bad ass four bedroom, three bathroom house with a huge swimming pool and deck area.

I pulled my ponytail tighter as I listened to Sinn go on and on about how Luck was probably going to send her back into the house to change. She said he was looney tune like that and didn't like for her to flaunt all of her juiciness in front of his niggas. I would be intimidated if I was an insecure bitch. But baby, I was secure in mine. Cass don't be checking for shit by Ms. Ryann.

We walked out onto the patio and the strong aroma of some good ass weed filled my nostrils. Cass, Luck, Wavy, and a couple other cats I noticed from the hood were standing by the barbeque pit where Luck was grilling some steaks. Tee Grizzley's 'No Effort' blasted from the big speakers sitting by the pool, where me and Sinn's drinks sat waiting for us.

Get your sack took, we gon' take you for a joke
If you like that last batch, bring some money take some mo'
Wanna take 'em to the 8, don't know which route I wanna take it
The country wait four years, we take presidents every day, nigga

One thing I can say about Luck and Sinn is that they had great hospitality. We were all just kicking it, there wasn't any occasion, but the way the music was blasting, drinks were floating, and blunts in rotation, you would think it was.

I sat on the side of the pool and stared at Cassim who was sitting across the backyard with his dark tinted shades on, antisocial as usual. I had to be staring at him for about five minutes before he smiled and nodded at me. Creepy ass had been staring at me the whole time, too. I shied away before blowing a kiss at him.

"You got that nigga so open," said Sinn sitting next to me, dipping her toes in the pool. "I ain't never seen Cass this way and I've known him for over ten years honey."

"He's got me open too," I said in return, blushing like a fuckin' school girl.

"Look at chu," said Sinn, leaning forward to get a good look at the smile on my face. "I sholl hope I get to be in the wedding. I know we just met and all, but in a few months, I'll be somethin' like a bestie."

I laughed and she continued, "No, for real though. I'm dope as fuck." She popped her lips and laughed.

Sinn was cool and down to earth, but I'm not a friendly bitch, and it takes more than a few months for me to truly bond with females. Plus, the best friend slot is already filled. At least, I hoped it still was.

I picked my cup up and took a few sips from it before easing my body down into the cold water. It was just what I needed on this hot ass day. I swear it had to be about one hundred degrees. Before we came out today, Cass's black ass put on sunscreen, talking about he didn't need the sun to burn him anymore than it already has.

Thoughts of Cassim flooded my mind all day, every day. A bitch was legit addicted to him. If I was away from him, I wondered what he was doing. And while I was with him, I wondered what he was thinking. Sinn was sitting a couple of inches away from me, running her big ass mouth, but all I could do was think about Cassim.

This shit is unhealthy. To love someone this much, knowing that one day they have to die is insane. I didn't even want to think about death when it came to Cass, but I did, and when I did, I didn't like it. It gave me anxiety. I hated that I had allowed myself to love someone so much that the mere thought of them being out of my life permanently, petrified me.

Sometimes I found myself obsessing over it. Wondering what I would do. Wondering if I would ever be able to function after it. Imagining how it would happen. Every time it ended in a blood bath. A blood bath that Cass didn't seem to care about. He didn't care about anything, but me. He didn't even care about himself, and sometimes, I thought that maybe that is where the overwhelming fear of losing him came into place.

"Ryann," said Sinn, snapping me out of my thoughts.

"Yeah," I replied.

"I was saying... my sister and a few of my girls are coming over—

"And I'm about to dip," I said with a chuckle. "I don't do new chicks, Sinn."

"I'm a new bitch and you 'did me'," she said with a frown of confusion. "Pause on that though."

I laughed and looked away from her just to get an eyeful of a group of half-naked bitches coming into the backyard. One in particular couldn't keep her fuckin' eyes off my nigga's dick print.

"Oh shit, there they go," said Sinn, standing up from the cement. "Ryann... you gone come say hi?"

I heard her. But my attention was fixed on the bitch who was boldly eye fucking my man. I mean, the backyard was full of niggas, but she just had to pick mine out of the bunch to eye fuck? I told that nigga not to wear those fuckin' basketball shorts out of the house a long time ago.

I climbed the brick stairs to the pool, steady looking over at them. Cassim was minding his own business, as usual, chopping it up with his niggas. But this bitch... she was steady looking at him. And when she leaned over to whisper something to the ho next to her, I walked off.

I scratched the side of my nose as I powerwalked right by Sinn, up to Cassim, who was pulling from a blunt. He inhaled a thick cloud of smoke and wrapped his hand around my waist cupping my ass.

I leaned closer to his ear and whispered, "What I tell you about these thin ass basketball shorts? You got ho's eye fucking you like I won't snatch the eyeballs out a bitch's head."

He pulled me closer to his body and said, "Why you worried about what mafuckas lookin at? Who's getting this dick though, sweetheart?"

"I told you, that's not the point. I just don't like it," I said with a scowl on my face.

Cassim was fronting like he didn't snap on niggas every time they looked at me the wrong way or said something out of the way. He was the same way about me, I was just a little more out there with my crazy. All Cassim had to do was give a look or say a few words, with little emotion behind it.

"Ryann, this is my sister, Symphony, my best friend, Cola, and my other two friends, Candy and Quisha," said Sinn from behind.

"Have fun Ry. None of that nutty shit, aight?" said Cassim after lifting his glasses from his eyes and locking eyes with me.

I rolled my eyes and grabbed his dick and said, "You need to go put some fuckin' jeans on, nigga. But aight."

He laughed and kissed me on the lips before I pulled away from him.

I turned around and gave the ladies a phony smile, "Hey."

"Ryann is Cass's fine ass girlfriend," said Sinn with a sly smile. "She got him wrapped around all of her fingers. Ain't that right, Cass?"

Cassim just lightly chuckled and continued to pull from his blunt paying us no attention. The girls all had surprised looks on their faces, and immediately went to checking me out. I swear, all of their eyes roamed my body.

"Nice to meet you, Ryann girl. You got one of the most wanted niggas around these parts," said the girl Cola with a laugh.

I didn't find her remark funny and just snorted before walking away to get back into the pool. I heard Sinn whisper that I was cool, but I wasn't good with meeting new people. Nah, I just wasn't good with meeting new bitches who obviously wanted to fuck my dude. I was only cordial with Sinn because she was with Luck. I still didn't trust her. I didn't trust any damn body.

"How long you and Cassim been talking?" asked Sinn's sister.

She was being cute. Using his real name, trying to make a statement. Most likely she's a bitter ass ex, trying to prove something to a bitch who couldn't give a fuck about her.

"How long you and Cassim been broken up?" I asked with a smirk as I took a sip of my drink.

She narrowed her eyes at me and then smiled, "Touché."

I don't play with bitches, so I didn't return the smile. I looked away and lowered my body down into the water. I didn't care about getting my hair wet because I was rocking my real hair. Being Puerto Rican and black had its perks. I sholl wish I knew a lot of my native language, because I've always wanted to cuss a bitch out in Spanish, talking all fast and shit. Petty. I know.

When I came up for air, Cassim was kneeling at the side of the pool, waiting for me. I walked closer to the side and he ran his big hands over my wet curly hair, "I've gotta shoot a move, gorgeous."

My eyebrows knitted together, "What? Why? Where are you about to go?" I asked. I looked around the backyard, "I don't know these people like that."

He chuckled and kissed me on the forehead, "Climb out."

I maneuvered around the pool to get to the stairs. He met me there and held his hand out for me to grab when I finally did get out. I could feel eyes on me, but I didn't care. I knew that Sinn's friends were watching me. I knew that her sister—clearly his ex—was watching too. An ex he failed to mention.

"Walk with me," he said as he handed me my towel.

I slipped my Gucci slides on and walked out of the backyard with him.

"Why didn't you tell me Sinn's sister was your ex?" I asked.

"Because it's not of importance, Ryann. Shorty's not even my ex, on some real shit. I fucked with her when I was younger. She was my first and all that. We fucked. She caught feelings. I ended things," he nonchalantly ran down to me. "Shorty's a true ass nutcase."

"That's all?" I asked with raised eyebrows.

"That. Is. All," he said with a smile. "I'm riding with Luck. You can take the whip whenever you're ready to go."

He grabbed my hands and interlocked his fingers with mine.

"Where you about to go," I asked as he kissed my knuckles.

"To check on a few operations. I'll be home later on tonight," he said in between kisses.

I had this nigga open. Do you hear me? He was standing in the driveway of his best friend's house, literally kissing my knuckles while them niggas stood a few feet away waiting on him, watching it all go down.

Cassim was such a grown ass man. He didn't care about public affection. He didn't care about showing people how much he cared about me. I loved how he was a totally different person when I wasn't within reach. He would sit back, with his glasses on, like he was the only man on earth. He was so unfazed by the conversations around him. Just laid back and chill.

But when I was within reach. When he could touch me. He never stopped. He couldn't keep his hands or lips off of me. I fucking loved it.

*

I smelled him before I saw him. Daddy was home.

I looked over my shoulder and out walked Cassim with his long dreads hanging over his shoulders. He must have undid them as soon as he walked into the house. He wanted to paralyze my ass. He wanted my infatuation to get the best of me.

He eased up behind me and wrapped his arms around my body. I deeply inhaled and closed my eyes, loving the scent of him suffocating me, loving the feel of him on my body. Butterflies filled my stomach as I began to feel the warmth of his peppermint scented breath on the nape of my neck while the shutter of my camera sounded. I was standing on the balcony taking pictures of the sunset.

My hands were a bit shaky as I tried to get a good capture. My throat felt a little dry when his lips met the small area behind my ear. Sometimes, he still had that effect on me. I couldn't even focus on the beauty in front of me because of the beauty that stood behind me. I started to turn around and he told me not to. He told me to take my pictures. But how could I? I wanted one of him. I wanted more of him... with his hair hanging looking like God's greatest creation. I needed more pictures of him. For when we grew old and gray. To remind me of what use to be. To remind me of the times where I was overly obsessed with this man I often called my King. My black, strong, sexy King.

I swallowed and licked my lips, as I tried to steady my hands for a picture. I couldn't and he sensed it, so he placed his hands on top of mine to steady them. I sighed, a heavy, breathy sigh when his hands touched mine.

"You aight, sweetheart?"

I shook my head no and he chuckled. He loved the affect he had on me. Sometimes he did this type of shit on purpose.

Finally, I got the perfect picture of the sun setting, and as soon as I did, I quickly turned around and pressed my lips against his.

He held me in his arms and lowered his strong hands down over my ass, "I love it when you get like this."

I laid my head on his shoulder with my eyes closed.

"What else do you love, Cassim?"

I still hadn't heard those three words and it was really starting to annoy me.

He cleared his throat and said, "You know what else—

"Knowing it and hearing it are two different things. Tell me, baby."

He held me tighter and was silent for a few seconds before saying, "I love you, sweetheart."

I melted. I fucking melted. Those foreign words sounded as sweet as honey slipping off his thick, succulent lips. Straight had a bitch all emotional and what not. I blushed, and he did too, but he quickly looked away.

I grabbed his chin to make him look me in the eyes, "Love is okay, Cassim."

He didn't say anything, but in his eye contact, I could see that he wasn't use to love.

"It is okay to love me, baby. I'm not... I'm not going anywhere."

He pulled away from my touch with a snort like he didn't believe me. I needed to know what was up with him and love. I understand, being an orphan can fuck your trust up, but didn't the family he was sent to, love him? Had Cassim ever been loved?

I grabbed his hand as he tried to walk away, "Stop. Talk to me."

"Nothing to talk about, gorgeous," he replied, gently touching my chin, and forcing a smile that he thought was going to shut me up like it usually does.

Nah, I was tired of tiptoeing around his feelings. I was tired of being in the dark. I needed to know more about him.

"Enough. Talk to me," I said as I grabbed his hand and sat him down on one of the chairs that sat on the balcony.

I sat in his lap and said, "You know everything about me. Yet, I know so little about you. I never tripped because I wanted to give you time, but enough time has passed and I need to know what it is that has you crying in your sleep. I need to know who—

He made a 'psssh' sound and sighed heavily, his ripped chest rising and falling, "C'mon shorty."

"Opening up won't do anything but make us closer, Cassim."

"I have nightmares, aight? I don't know why, but them shits came back," he reluctantly admitted with a scowl on his face.

"Nightmares about what? What do you mean they came back?"

Cassim then took a deep breath and grabbed hold of my hand.

He told me how his mother abandoned him. How he went from foster home to foster home. He told me about the horrible things he had to do to eat and to drink. He told me he didn't learn to talk until he was five years old. Said his ma was a crackhead who only called him mothafucka, so he only answered to that for so long. He said that everything was straight until he was forced to leave his first foster parents due to him being too difficult for them to care for him and his PTSD. He said that after he left them, he was practically back at square one.

"That...that I don't want to even talk about," he sternly said with flaring nostrils.

I left it alone. I didn't say anything, actually. I wrapped my arms around him and just held him. No child should have had to go through what he went through. Now I got it. I understood why he cared so much about children. And as that realization sat in, guilt crept upon me.

That baby I killed. The one I aborted... it could have been his. I never wanted him to find out about that abortion. It would kill him, and definitely kill our relationship. I planned on taking that secret to the grave. But life... life has fucked up way of bringing secrets into the light. But that's another scene, for another chapter.

"I love you, Cassim. I love you so fucking much," I said, breaking the awkward silence

He kissed the top of my head, "I know."

I nudged him a little and he said, "I love you too, sweetheart."

Chapter Nine . Cass

"I told you I could flip shit, nigga," said Juice sitting across from me, chiefing on a cigarette.

I looked down into the duffle bag full of money with raised eyebrows, "You a dope boy na, bruh?"

Juice ran his free hand over the top of his head, "Man nah, I just needed something to get me on my feet. Shit smooth now. I'm going back to murkin' niggas on a regular." He pointed at me, "You need a couple heads split?"

I looked up at him with a smirk, "Nah. I got everything I need right chea."

I was surprised at Juice coming through with my portion, and even a few stacks for himself in such a short period of time. I just knew I was going to spray off on the nigga. But nah, he pulled through.

"Who you serve to," I asked as I rested back against the worn leather sofa of the trap.

"The Bag Boys," he said with a smirk. "Only reason I asked you to front me the shit because I knew them niggas were looking for work."

I nodded and zipped the duffle bag up, "So, you got them niggas pushing my work on their blocks?"

"If you get out of your feelings, it could be a profitable ass business deal, my baby," Juice said with a smile.

Dawg was sitting across from me smirking, like I was against the idea. I was all for it. I never took business personal. But I highly doubt it if Mr. Clean would keep copping if he knew it was coming from me.

"Why do you want out already, G," I asked as I slid the duffle bag over to the side of the couch.

He leaned forward and put his cigarette out in the ashtray, "I kill niggas. I don't push dope. I just saw an easy lick... jumped on it... and came out with a few bands."

I rubbed my beard, with my mouth slightly turned down, "You can make a shit load more if you keep serving to them niggas."

Juice clasped his hands together, visibly taking what I was proposing into consideration. He cocked his head to the side a little and asked me what kind of deal I was putting on the table.

I licked my lips, "You moved that product fast as hell. And eventually they'll be calling for more because my shit is just that fuckin' good." I paused, "I want you to keep servin' them niggas. Keep hitting them off with good product and in exchange, you'll get to keep five percent."

He snorted, "Five? Come on bruh."

I shrugged, "Five percent is better than the zero you'll be left with if I get one of my young dawgs to do it."

He smirked and said, "Aight, nigga. I'm with it."

We shook hands and parted ways.

*

"Your total is one hundred and forty-five dollars, beautiful," said the cashier at Footlocker like I wasn't standing right next to Ryann.

She glanced at me with a smirk as she fished money from her purse. I stepped in front of her and went into my pocket to pay for the shoes she was buying. I glanced up at the cashier and he was busy staring at Ryann.

"Eyes over here, nigga," I said with the jerk of my head.

He cleared his throat and smiled before running his hand over his mouth.

"You want me to embarrass you in front of this beautiful ass woman, my mans?" I asked him as I peeled two hundred dollars off.

"What?" he asked with furrowed eyebrows.

Ryann wrapped her arms around me from behind and whispered, "Be nice."

I scratched the tip of my nose, "She's beautiful, right? Nice to look at, ain't she?"

The sales associated turned his top lip up and said, "I didn't mean any disrespect—

"And I won't mean any when I knock ya eyes out cha skull. Bag this shit up, bruh."

I could tolerate Ryann being looked at my random niggas. I mean, listen, the shit is expected, baby is fucking gorgeous. But he was boldly flirting with her like he'd lost all of the sense the good Lord gave him.

He chuckled and finished the transaction. I snatched the bag up and said, "Have a blessed day, boy."

Ryann bumped me with her hip and tried to pry the bag out of my hands.

"Stop playing with me, sweetheart. You already tried to pull money out yo purse... stop acting like I let shit like that fly."

"The shoes are for my brother. You didn't have to buy them."

I didn't say anything else. Ryann thought it was about the fact that she was buying shoes for Adrien. I never wanted Ryann to have to pay with anything. She told me about her goals. She told me how she wanted to get a photography studio... all that... so whatever she made from photography, I wanted her to save up for it.

Of course, I've offered to pay for the studio, but she was adamant about getting it herself. Independence and shit. So, I respected it.

*

After kicking it at the mall with shorty, I had to link with Scotty about the group home. I was happy to hear that my application had been approved and that I could move on to the next step in the process. Renovations and hiring was what was next. A nigga was dead ass excited. I don't think I've ever been this excited about anything in my life and that was pretty fuckin' sad if you thought about it.

I pulled up at the property before Scotty did just to bask in my mafuckin glory. I still hadn't told anybody about this. I didn't know why but I still wasn't ready to share the news with anybody. Some thing on my spirit wasn't sitting right. I felt like something was going to go wrong. That feeling came from never having shit. I mean, I've got a lot, but nothing like this. Nothing good and pure like this. I felt like God was going to snatch this mafucka right away from me like *'you don't deserve this shit, you heathen.'* I was a wretched soul. I knew this, but I felt like... this right here would right my wrongs in some way.

I sat on the hood of my whip and cracked the bottle of Ace of Spade open. I looked up at the building— that needed a lot of fuckin' restoration might I add—with a smirk as I put the bottle up to my lips.

Mafuckas warranted me a lost cause. Said I was never going to be shit but a crack baby. I was put through a lot growing up. So much that I started to believe what they said about me. The system was no good to me. Nothing to me. It took me rising above that stereotype to

overcome the obstacles. I sold drugs, I murdered folks...
all that. But what bad was I really doing?

The drugs I sold, I sold to mafuckas who wanted it.
I didn't force it upon 'em. And the murdering? I gave that
to mafuckas who wanted it too.

Minutes later, Scotty pulled up. He hopped out of
his Lamborghini with a grin on his face, carrying a gift
bag. We slapped hands and I nodded down at the gift bag,
"Fucks that Scotty boy?"

He extended the bag to me, "Congratulations,
Cassim man. We did it."

I nodded and took the bag from him. He leaned
against my whip and I handed him the bottle of Ace of
Spades.

"Who would have thought man? Two hopeless
kids from the poorest part of Detroit. Lost in the system...
would finally be here man? I'm pushing a Lambo, with a
prestigious law firm. You... You sell a lil' dope but look at
what you got man? You're giving kids like us a fighting
chance. Something we didn't have growing up," said
Scotty before putting the bottle of Ace of Spade to his lips.

Yeah, you read that right. Scotty and I both grew
up in the system. I met him at Ms. Mable and Mr.
Gregory's group home. He was sent to Mr. Anne and Mr.
Tyrone's group home right before I slit Mr. Tyrone's
throat.

I looked down into the bag and shook my head,
"Fuck is this, Scotty?"

He laughed, "I framed the fucking approval letter.
Put that fucker on your mantle or something guy."

I tossed the gift bag through the open window of
my car, "Did they ask about the money?"

"Of course," he paused. "That inheritance from Ms.
Mable and Mr. Tyrone is still paying off."

I got an inheritance from Ms. Mable and Mr. Tyrone right before I started slanging dope. Them old people put me in their will. Left me over one hundred thousand dollars. Shits been gone, but to this day, I still claimed to be using it on the properties I bought.

Chapter Ten . Ryann

"Congratulations," I sang with a smile as I walked onto Hart Plaza, where I was meeting my clients.

I was finally out doing some work. This photoshoot was supposed to happen long ago, but since I was still going through the Dinero situation, I was forced to reschedule. These days I was in my best mood and could capture beauty out of the dullest sceneries. That time off did nothing but inspire me further. I was finally feeding my soul.

The bride to be unwrapped her arms from around her fiancé and turned to me, "Oh, thank you!"

When we locked eyes, I shook my head, about ready to turn away. But I'm all about my business. And it's always business before pleasure.

I extended my hand, approaching Symphony and her fiancé, "Nice to finally meet you."

She firmly shook my hand and said, "Likewise."

She was a bit uncomfortable and I couldn't understand why. Shit, I wasn't rude to her. I could have checked her about the way she was watching Cassim's dick print, but I didn't. I let the shit ride because I didn't want to upset him. What happened at the pool could have gone a lot worse.

I mumbled, "Lighten up. I'm here to do a job and I'm going to do it to the best of my ability."

She mumbled, "I don't have to worry about my photoshoot being sabotaged, do I?"

I looked at her like she was out of her fuckin mind, "What kind of woman do you take me for?"

"I don't know what kind of woman you are. You are involved with Cassim after all," she said through her teeth, with a smile on her face.

"Stop playing with me, Symphony. Don't make me drag yo ass all up and down the Riverwalk, sweetie."

She's the goofy bitch Cassim said she was. I would have never took this gig if I knew she was Mrs. Symphony Gibson to be. What the hell did she mean by that statement she made? She was once involved with him too. The fuck? She get a white dude and all of a sudden she's holier than thou. Fuck outta here.

Her fiancé approached us and shook my hand.

"Good afternoon, I'm Todd," he said introducing himself.

I smiled sweetly and shook it, "Ryann. Nice to meet you, Mr. Gibson."

"Please, call me Todd."

He still had my hand in his hand. He didn't pull his hand away until Symphony cleared her throat and pulled at his arm.

Her intimidation by me was ruining the photoshoot. We had finally began. They wanted pictures by the fountain, but Symphony's poses and smiles were so unnatural. I kept telling her to lighten up and just to be as natural as possible, but she was snappy. Snappy for what? I couldn't understand where her animosity came from. We barely spoke to each other at Sinn's house. The only time we exchanged words was when Sinn introduced us and she asked me who Cassim was. That is it.

Jealousy. That's all I could get from this situation.

"Please, Symphony. Just... pretend that you two are at home alone. Gaze into his eyes like you love—

"That is what I'm doing. I do love my fiancé, thank you. Maybe you need to back off with all of the direction and just take the fucking picture," she snapped.

I laughed and chewed on the inside of my cheeks to keep calm. I was getting frustrated and about ready to walk off. I even offered to give her, her deposit back since things weren't working out. I swear, I was being extra professional. The only time I stepped out of line was when I threatened to drag her down the Riverwalk. But since then... since we've officially gotten to work.. I've been nothing but professional.

Her disrespect got so wild that Todd had to apologize and ask for a few minutes alone with her. I stood there sipping from my cup of Iced Coffee, calm cool and collective, waiting. In their absence, I had about five people come up to me, complimenting me, asking for my card. They saw the lengths I went for a great photo. They saw me crouching. They saw me trying to hit Symphony and her husband from gorgeous angles. I even had a couple people apologize to me for Symphony's behavior. I kept a cool head on gigs for these reasons alone. We were in public. People could see me. Professionalism was a hustle. And I was always about my bread. I let Symphony talk crazy, because I had my camera out. People were watching.

Finally, they came back and Symphony had a better attitude.

"I apologize. Thank you for your patience," she said with a tight-lipped smile.

I nodded with a smile and said, "You're welcome."

The over posing didn't get better. It actually got worst. But did I say anything? Hell no, I didn't. I took the pictures with a smile and carried on with my day. Stiff ass bitch.

*

"Damn, bitch is Ashlee and Shaneka the only two people you see on this porch," I said to Omni before she walked into my house, following behind my brother.

The shoot was over and I had stopped over at the house to grab some more of my things. At this rate, I was thinking about getting a UHAUL. I never realized I had so much stuff. I thought I'd be able to just pack everything in my car and be done, since I wasn't taking any of the furniture or appliances. I didn't need to. I was going to a home with all of that, plus more. Cassim's house was like a damn castle. Bringing extra furniture would only cause clutter.

She rolled her eyes, and continued behind him.

I jumped up from my chair and followed them into the house, "Why in the fuck are y'all always at my shit? This bitch clearly don't fuck with me anymore. Take y'all asses to Bloomfield Hills."

"You keep throwing that bitch word around," said Omni with a chuckle.

"Yes, bitch, because you a fraud. How you cut me off because I didn't tell you that Juice was cheating on you? But yet, you still following behind his ass like a fucking child."

My feelings were hurt. I would never pop off on Omni like this is they weren't. But that shit burned me up when she walked up on my porch and spoke to everybody but me, yet she was still sucking and fuckin Juice like wasn't worth a damn.

"Chill out, Ry," said Juice. "I just came to grab some shit from the basement. Plus, you about to move. Shut yo mad ass up, girl."

"Shut up? No, nigga you shut up! So, what? It's still mine until I officially move out. What? You want to throw up the fact that you gave it to me too, Juice?"

"What? Man, chill," he replied with a frown. "Just chill we about to be gone."

"Chill? She's the disrespectful one! She can wait her fake ass in the car. Tuh," I said with a deadly scowl while Omni stood there with her arms crossed over her chest.

"I'm not going to be too many more of yo bitches, Ryann," she said with that same as chuckle like she was intimidating me.

"You gone be more than just a bitch if you don't get out of my house."

Granted, I was in the process of moving out, but it was still mine and would always be. So, what. So fucking what! It is mine until I leave. Period.

"Ryann," yelled Juice.

"Go sit in the car, my baby. I don't want to see y'all scrap man, come on," said Adrien coming from the back of the house.

"Don't talk to her, Adrien. Fuck wrong with you, nigga," yelled Juice.

Adrien walked right by Juice and told Omni to go into the car. Adrien was the nonchalant one of the trio. He was unbothered by shit and I loved that by him. He was so calm, cool, and collective that he barely even raised his voice. So, if Adri was ever loud and on tip, it was because someone really pushed him past his limit.

"Adri—

Adrien closed the storm door in response to Juice calling him. Not a fuck was given. He was doing more for Omni than her own nigga was. Because I swear on life she was a few seconds away from getting dragged.

It had been weeks since I heard anything from Omni. I couldn't believe she had really cut me off. She proved me right. Had I told her, all she would have done was stayed with him, so what was the point? She was being weak, letting him cheat and go upside her head. Now she had cut me off.. the only person who really cared about her in this whole situation.

"Gone outside, baby," said Juice to Omni.

Of course, she walked off. Stupid ass.

"You gone keep being his doormat huh," I said not caring shit about the way Juice was looking at me.

Omni didn't say anything. She kept out of the door and I followed behind her. Had she been anybody else, I would be sitting back, unfazed by her presence. But she was my best friend and she wasn't talking to me. I couldn't believe she was doing me like this. I wanted her to talk to me, but she just kept walking, which only pissed me off more. I was so tempted to grab her ponytail and beat her in the face, I was just that frustrated.

Juice was popping off too, telling me to mind my own business, but I was unbothered by his ass.

"Just get your shit so you and yo bonehead bitch can skate," I said before slamming the storm door. "Stupid ass bitch."

"Ryann—

"Shut up Nek. You see how this ho is doing me?"

"You know bitches choose dick over their besties all day. Stop acting so shocked."

We were talking about Omni like she wasn't walking down the stairs. And she kept walking. Didn't say anything to any of us.

"Fuck you Omniel, aight? After all we've gone through... this how you do me? Fake ass bitch... you were never a friend."

She stopped in her tracks, with her back to me. I could tell she was sighing by the rise and fall of her exposed shoulders. She could put up this tough façade all she wanted to. I knew that this was hurting her just as much as it was hurting me. I knew she needed me. I knew she needed someone to vent to about Juice's ass. Who had she been going to the nail salon with for her weekly mani and pedi? Who was she kicking it with every day? We stuck together like glue, but she was tearing our bond a part because I didn't want to tell her Juice was cheating? What the fuck?

She sighed again, "Stop calling me bitches, Ryann."

"Ry, leave her alone, my baby. Fuck," said Adri with a chuckle. "Shit ain't right, yo. Go kiss and make up."

"Fuck her," I said as I took my seat and pulled my phone out of my bra to delete her from my contacts. "Bitch."

She chuckled and shook her head, and then finally continued on to Juice's car.

I wanted to get a reaction out of her. I can admit that. I wanted her to come at me with some ol *'stop whining bitch, I still love your fake ass'* type of shit but she didn't. She got inside of the car and slammed the door.

Wow.

Chapter Eleven . Cass

"Babe... what's this?" asked Ryann, pulling the gift bag Scotty got me from the back seat.

I was pushing the UHAUL and she was pushing the whip. She was finally getting ready to move all of her shit in the crib. I was happy. Waking up to her every morning was about to be the highlight of my day. There was nothing like waking up to her smiling face.

I treaded to the whip, scratching the back of my ear, "Uhhh."

She pulled the framed letter of approval from the bag with furrowed eyebrows, "What is this?"

I grabbed it from her and stuffed it back inside of the bag, "Ain't nothing. I got a lil' property and shit."

She turned her head a little with that same frown, "Nothing? A lil property? Nothing is lil' about a property. And it must be a big deal. Scotty gifted a framed copy of the approval letter to you."

I licked my lips, "Property for a girl and boys home."

Her eyes shot up and a smile spread wide across her face, "Oh my God, baby! Why didn't you say anything?"

I shrugged, "Was waiting for shit to get into motion."

She squinted, "Ummm, things are in motion, Cass. This is amazing babe. Congratulations!"

I gave her a half smile and thanked her.

*

"What do you want to eat?" asked Ryann scrolling through an app on her phone for recipes. "I've been thinking about a butter and garlic shrimp scampi—

The sound of police sirens cut her off and she froze up. She looked over her shoulder, and grabbed my bicep. She had been petrified since she went to jail for that lil' bit. I pulled over on side of the road and rubbed her hand.

"Relax, sweetheart," I said as I looked through my rearview mirror.

Fuck did these niggas want? I was iffy about riding out so late to grab groceries so that she could cook because of the fuck shit the cops this way be on, but shorty gets what she wants. She expressed to me how she was tired of eating fast food and felt like we needed to eat in more. I didn't blame her for me getting pulled over at all. I blamed my black skin, and the fact that ninety percent of white cops are racist. I was doing the exact speed limit, and everything on my whip was legit, so the fuck were they pulling me over for?

"I need you to step out of the vehicle, sir," said the cop standing at my lowered window with one hand on his pistol, and the other wrapped around the flashlight he had in my face.

It was like Déjà vu. Ryann was sitting next to me and standing at her window was another cop.

"For what?" I asked unmoving.

Ryann sighed, "Please, Cassim."

She wanted me to comply like complying would save my life if they decided to kill me. I had every right to ask what they wanted since they had absolutely no legit reason for pulling me over.

I took my sunglasses off and handed them to her before unbuckling my seatbelt. Because she wanted me to chill, I decided to do just that.

I stepped out of the car, and the cop threw me against the car and placed my hands behind my back.

"Let him go," yelled Ryann at the top of her lungs. "Why are you doing this? You didn't even tell us why you pulled us over!"

"I'm going to have to ask you to remain silent," said the officer next to her window.

The officer on me pressed his elbow into my back, and I smiled, "Yo, watch ya fuckin' aggression, my mans, and tell me what the fuck you pulling me over for?"

I didn't fuck with the Mosley's, but for this nigga here, I would call 'eem up. Let them niggas get pig blood on 'em.

"You're wanted for questioning in regards to a murder. You have the right to remain silent. Anything you say can and will be used against you in a court of law. You have the right to an attorney. If you cannot afford an attorney, one will be appointed for you..."

"Murder," yelled Ryann from the inside of the car. "He didn't do anything," she screamed.

"Hands on the dashboard," yelled the officer standing at her window with his gun drawn. "One more sudden movement and I'm going to light your black ass up."

"Ryann... sweetheart... relax. It's cool baby. It's cool," I said as the cop behind me put my handcuffs on too fuckin' tight. "I'll be home in a couple hours."

I prayed like hell that, that was a word I'd be able to keep.

Chapter Twelve . Ryann

Again. I was without him... a-fucking-gain.

And this time, I felt like it would be forever. It had been two days. He told me he would be right back... but that wasn't the case. It had been two fucking days without him, and in those two days, I've eaten absolutely nothing. All I've done in those two days were lie in his bed, unmoving. I couldn't do anything, but think about the last time I saw him, and the reassurance in his voice when he told me everything would be okay.

How?

He didn't know what his disappearance did to me last time. How it destroyed me. How it paralyzed me. How the birds stopped singing and how the sun stopped shining. He didn't know. I told him. But he didn't know. He couldn't feel what I felt.

Because now... now felt permanent.

Now could be forever. Since his altercation with Dinero's parents that day, people thought that he was the one that killed them. We didn't know who in the hood had even mentioned it. Someone said that a tall dark skin man with dreadlocks was arguing with the McGee's before they were brutally murdered. All they had was speculation. No evidence. No testimony. Nothing. So.. so why wasn't he here? I felt helpless at this point.

Now could very well be permanent. The realization... the emptiness I felt... the paralyzing fear of it... made me feel weak. I would die without Cassim. I thought that staring at his pictures would make me feel better. But it didn't. Staring at his pictures made me feel worst. Staring at his pictures made me want him more.

In the darkness, my phone rang, but would go unanswered if it was not him.

And it wasn't.

It was Ashlee.

They were worried about me because of the state I was in the last time they seen me.

Silent. Crying. Destroyed. In denial.

I was a wreck when they picked me up from the hospital. Yes... the hospital. The police officers took me to the hospital because they thought I was mentally ill. Without Cassim, I was. Life couldn't just go back to normal after having him. I could not be strong. I could not just go on with my life. Not after what I had with him. Not after everything we've experienced. Not after every mind-blowing orgasm, every smile, every kiss, the laughter... the secrets we've shared. Life could not just go on. How? How when him and I had become life to each other?

I turned over on my back and stared up at the ceiling.

Unmoving, with tears sliding down the sides of my face. And then a smile, brought on by memories of him, crept upon my face. Memories of the real reason he never stepped foot inside of a pool. He had one of his own and never used it because secretly, he could not swim. One day, I forced him to get inside with me. It took me diving in completely naked to get him inside. Everything was fine until I forced him to the deep end of the pool. He slipped and lost his balance. It was then that I figured it out.

Watching him struggle, thinking he was dying...it cracked me the hell up. I helped him though. I pulled his heavy ass right to the staircase where he lied in my arms, breathing heavy with a face full of water. I cracked jokes on him that whole day.

I missed him.

I missed him so much.

The doorbell rang and I grabbed the remote from the nightstand to see who it could be. It was Luck. He had been here to check on me every day. I'd answer and tell him I was fine. Today when I answered, he didn't walk away when I told him I was okay.

"What," I said to him as he stood there at the door, unmoving.

"Bro want me to get a good look at you."

"I said I'm fine, Luck," I snapped.

But I wasn't fine. I had bags underneath my eyes and my hair was all over my head. I probably had an odor seeping from my pores too, since I hadn't bathe in those two days. I've been right here, in this bed. The only time I got up was to use the bathroom and to get a few sips of water from the bathroom sink. I hadn't been out of this room since I've been here.

He sighed, "But he wants me to see you. Ya peoples talking.. saying their worried about you."

I sighed and said, "Go away-

"I'm not leaving until you open the door, Ry," he sternly replied with his thick eyebrows raised.

I turned the video and intercom off and tried to will myself out of bed. Finally, I stood up and sluggishly went into the bathroom to brush my hair and teeth. I sniffed underneath my arms, and it was tart as fuck under there. Smelled like a chili dog with extra onions. I didn't care though. I carried my ass right down stairs.

I unlocked the locks and opened the door up. I stood in between the little space between the cracked door and the door frame, not allowing him to come in.

"Happy now?"

"Do you need anything? Food, money, anything," he asked. "Turn the porch light back on, Ry."

Yeah, I turned it off. I didn't want him to see how distraught I was. Mosley's are known for being strong... and usually I am... but when it comes to missing Cassim, I'm weak.

"I don't need anything. I have my own money and I've eaten already," I lied. "And for what? I can see you perfectly clear."

"Ain't nobody about to play with this damn girl," I heard Sinn say before their car door slammed.

She marched up towards the house and pushed her way past Luck. Bitch was so bold, that she literally pushed herself into the house too. I tried to hold the door closed, but Sinn's a big bitch and knocked me right out of the way. She looked over her shoulder at Luck, "I'll be home in the morning, aight?"

He nodded and walked down the steps.

"Bitch, you must be out of your mind," I yelled.

She flicked the foyer light on and looked me up and down, "And you must be sick in the head. What the hell is wrong with you, Ryann? You really up in this dark ass house on some ol' gothic shit smelling like a patty melt with extra onions? Bitch you the one out of yo mind."

I couldn't even get mad. I actually cracked a smile. It was the first one since I'd talked to him yesterday morning.

Sinn closed the door behind her, and walked further into the house, shaking her head full of faux locs, "You really out here bad like this because that nigga been locked up for a couple hours? Girl," she rolled her eyes. "Luck did a whole year and I still kept my shit together. Now, I don't know you that well, or where yo mental headspace is at but, I'ma just assume you got some kind of issues."

I laughed. I literally cracked up laughing. From the outside looking in, I did look bat shit crazy and that was because people didn't know. They saw all the cutesy shit and how I'd flip on a bird for staring...but they didn't know. They didn't know about the pictures I took of him. They didn't' know about my infatuation. They just thought it was love. But it was deeper than love. I was addicted to Cassim, and right now... I was going through withdrawals.

Sinn laughed as she spoke, "I'm forreal, girl. I just don't know. This type of behavior ain't normal."

I rolled my eyes and asked her what she wanted.

"For starters, I want you to shower and scrub underneath those arms. I'm happy I put a smile on your face, but Ryann...I need you to cheer up. What else besides Cass makes you happy?"

Photography.

But nothing photographed right without him.

"Photography. I'm a photographer," I replied as I wrapped my arms around my body.

"Well, hell, get out and take some pictures, Ryann. You've gotta do something other than lying up in this dark ass castle, alone, crying, and stinking."

Did she think I wanted to be like this? I didn't. My brothers had called and left several voice mails and text messages about how weak I was being, telling me to grow some balls and hold the nigga down. But I couldn't shake this depression. People on the outside looking in thought I was overreacting, and maybe I was. But I still couldn't control it. I missed him and I felt like I would miss him forever if they didn't get a handle on the situation.

The fucked up part about all of this was that Cassim really was innocent. He didn't look innocent because everyone had seen him barge into Dinero's parents house. They heard the gunshot. But no one was hit. They saw and heard everything that could have very well led to him killing the whole family. At this point, it didn't matter what he didn't do. What mattered was what it looked like he had done.

I sat on the couch and shook my head, "I can't, Sinn."

Sinn kneeled in front of me, looking me in the eyes, "I swear to God I've never seen anything like this. You loved that black ass nigga for real huh?"

I looked off and blinked tears away, "More than anybody can understand."

This thing with Cassim. It happened well before he had a voice. Before I felt his rough hands on my soft skin. Well before his full lips were upon mine. I've had feelings for him before I even knew him. And now... now that I've heard his voice. Felt his hands on my soft skin, and now that I've felt those fat lips on me... my feelings for him had only grown stronger. I loved Cassim with all of me. I didn't just speak those three words—I meant them. I felt them.

"That niggas dick must be coated in gold," she said with a giggle.

I didn't find shit funny about her mentioning his dick.

"The only dick you should be worried about is Luck's—not Cassim's," I snapped, locking eyes with her.

She drew back and said, "Girl I'm just saying."

It wasn't about sex. It was the way he made me feel. It was the way he looked at me. It was the way he touched me. The way he spoke... his flaws... the perfections about him that he saw as imperfections. It was just Cassim.

I pushed myself up from the couch, and started to the stairs for a shower, "I'm about to shower, Sinn. You don't have to babysit me."

"Don't forget about what I said about those sour ass armpits. I'm about to fix you something to eat."

*

The next morning, I woke up to a call from him.

After getting past the operator, a smile spread wide as all outside upon my face when I heard his voice.

"Good morning, sweetheart."

I moaned. Yes, I fucking moaned.

"Good morning, baby," I cooed. "When are you coming home? Why haven't your lawyer gotten you out yet—

"Slow down, baby," he said cutting me off. "Take a deep breath and calm down."

I did. I took a deep breath, but I did not calm down. I was anxious. I needed him. I wanted him here with me. I wanted to wake up to the smell of his bitter breath. I wanted to feel his scruffy facial hair on the nape of my neck. I did not want to wake up to a phone call. I wanted to wake up buried in his arms, nearly suffocating by the way he held on to me.

"When," I said, hoping to hear some good news.

"In a bit," he replied.

I screamed. Yes, I fucking screamed.

"Yeeeeees. Oh my God," I jumped out of bed and bumped my knee against the nightstand. "I'm...I'm about to throw some pajama pants on and come right down—

"Luck is coming to get me, Ry. I want you to make me some of them fiy ass pancakes. A nigga is in need of a good home cooked meal."

I nodded rapidly like he could see me, "Yes, got damnit. Yes. Whatever you want, King. I'm about to cook them shits ass naked. You gone have food and pussy waiting on a platter for you, nigga."

Cassim cracked up laughing. He called me crazy and said that he just wanted to let me know that he would be home soon, so that I would stop acting crazy. He wanted me to go out and take some pictures of the clouds. He knew. He knew I had been cooped up in this house, doing nothing...letting my camera sit there untouched. Luck told him because Sinn had told him.

"Alright. I love you, Cassim," I gushed as I stood there twiddling my hair.

"I love you too, sweetheart," He said with a smile in his voice.

After we hung up, I showered, dried off and literally cooked breakfast ass naked. I was not playing with him. I went all out too. I cooked pancakes, waffles, sausage patties and sausage links, grits—and I wasn't even sure if he ate those—, cheesy eggs, hash browns, and I cut up some fruit.

I had to check my makeup like ten times, reapplied oil to my body, and sprayed on Chanel number five about three times before I heard his keys at the door. I stood at the foyer, with my arms stretched out across the doorway waiting with my ass slightly poked out to the side. My heart was beating nearly out of my chest. I was so excited, that I'm sure I wouldn't be able to stand here when he finally got inside.

As soon as he got inside, he took me in with wide eyes, and his bottom lip between his teeth.

"Welcome home, King," I said before letting go of the walls and jumping into his arms.

He stumbled back into the storm door with a chuckle. I cupped his face in my hands and said, "I missed you. I missed your perfect face. This forehead," kiss. "this nose," Kiss. "These cheeks," kiss, kiss. "And above all things... these fucking lips," Kiss.

He parted my lips with his tongue and our tongues did the tango. I wrapped my arms around his neck, and he held onto me tightly as we both intensified the kiss. He grabbed a handful of my ass and pulled me closer to his body. His dick was rock hard, and pulsating against my thigh, driving me right at the edge of insanity. Good God I missed this nigga.

"What about this monstrous mafucka," he whispered in my ear.

I gripped his dick and moaned before biting my bottom lip, "Oh you know good and got damn well I missed him."

"*Ahem*,"

The sound of someone clearing their throat, grabbed both of our attention. That same white bitch from a while ago stood in the door, holding on to what looked like an apple pie or some shit.

I placed my hands on my lips and asked, "You need something?"

Yes, bitch, I stood there as naked as the day I was born, not giving a damn. She pursed her lips together, looked down at her feet, and then back up at us.

"I brought pie," she said with a smile.

Cassim let me go, and turned around, "Go home, Jane."

Her eyes averted between Cassim and I, as she shuffled her feet like she just couldn't walk away. I looked up at Cassim with furrowed eyebrows and asked him what was up with this broad. He grabbed at his earlobe and told 'Jane' to go home again.

"Is she your girlfriend? Is she why you're not responding to my advances, Cass," she boldly asked.

I chuckled and started to say something, but Cassim cut me off.

"Listen darlin," he sighed. "You sucked my dick. That's it. You got a whole ass husband at home, Jane. Go home to my man's Billy."

She shifted again and rubbed her nose with her freehand.

With a harsh whisper she said, "But you're all I've been thinking about! You don't shove that thing down my throat and just...not fuck me with it now."

"Get rid of that bitch, Cass. We missed you," I told him, as I motioned at my most sexual places.

*

"So, what happened babe," I asked, as I laid my naked ass on the kitchen floor, sticky from the syrup he'd poured all over my body. "What are they saying?"

Cassim sucked on my sweet skin in between every word he spoke, "A bunch of bullshit. Talm'bout I fit the description of someone who'd had an altercation with them just hours before. They tried to place me at the scene and all that. I spent most of my time in the interrogation room."

"Where was Scotty? If they didn't have any evidence, why did they keep you for so long, Cassim? You sure ain't nobody snitching? We gotta end this shit before—

He laughed and cut me off, "Chill, sweetheart. The shit is under control. Scotty was there. They wouldn't let 'em back, talking about some ol' technical difficulties type bullshit. They didn't let him back until this morning, G drawing up a lawsuit right now." He rubbed his lips against my shoulder, "No one is talking. No one is stupid enough. Mafuckas know I'll snatch their whole fuckin' mug off behind some shit like that. Straight skin a mafucka alive."

I shuddered a little, and just cuddled closer to him.

"You sure," I asked, a little worried.

"I'm positive."

*

I didn't want to let Cassim out of my sight after being away from him for so long. It might not seem long to you, but listen... I thought I lost my baby fa eva.

He had some business to take care of and since I respected that, I let him handle his. I had to finish moving in, anyway. I still had a lot of stuff back at the house to grab so I decided to busy myself by piling some more things into my little car. I didn't drive the UHAUL because that thing was big and scary.

I parked my car in the driveway and hopped out. As usual, the block was slapping, and my porch was crowded. Ashlee, Nek, Omniel, Juice, Goose, and a couple of other people were posted up, talking and laughing. I hadn't been home in about three days, so when I walked up on the porch, all conversation seized and they hit me with questions I knew they'd been dying to ask.

"Damn bitch, you straight up disappeared on us. I thought we were going to have to send a search party out for you," said LeeLee with a smirk. "You aight?"

That bitch knew I was at Cassim's house losing my mind, shutting myself off from the rest of the world. Petty drunk bitch wanted me to say such, but I smiled and kept up the stairs. I gave Goose's shoulder a light squeeze before speaking to him.

Our relationship had always been a little rocky, because the nigga dead ass terrified me. But since he flipped out, saying that I didn't care about him and all that, I've been a lot nicer.

Yeah, he thought I hated him because of what he did to the McGee's. I tried to explain to Goose that it wasn't that I didn't like him, he just terrified me. You would think he understood that considering how I found him that night, surrounded by candles and shit. But Gooses' mind didn't work like that. Sometimes, he had the mind of a child, and sometimes he had the mind of a monster. Right now, I got the in between Goose.

"What's good, Ry Baby," he asked with a smile that mirrored our fathers. "You smooth? My nigga Cass... he smooth?"

I smiled and nodded, "Yep. Everything is all good."

"That's why you smiling, huh?" said Nek with a cup up to her mouth. "Only that nigga makes you happy anymore."

I squinted at her and just walked into the house. I was in a gravy ass mood and did not want to deal with Nek and her jealousy right now. Every time I saw that bitch she was green with envy. It was starting to annoy the fuck out of me, to be honest. At this point, it was in Nek's best interest to stay thee fuck away from me.

Ten minutes into packing up more of my things there was a knock at my bedroom door. I rolled my eyes, just knowing it was Nek.

But to my surprise, it wasn't.

It was Omni.

She peeked her head inside and said, "Hey best friend."

I rolled my eyes, "Psssh, bitch please."

She walked further into the room and sat on my bed, "Ryann, I miss you."

I glanced from my duffle bag, and then at her, "Whatever Omni. You straight up flipped on me."

She looked down at the floor and said, "I've been a mess.... A complete mess. This thing with Juice... it's fucking with me in ways that I never thought imaginable. I feel trapped, Ryann. Trapped and alone. Especially since you and I haven't been talking. I didn't realize how much I needed you."

I laughed and looked up at the ceiling, "How much you needed me? Omni.. are you fucking hearing yourself?!" I yelled. "I got raped! Raped and had a fucking abortion! No one seemed to give a fuck. Nobody but my brothers, and Cassim. The rest of you bitches," I waved her off. "You ho's straight sided with Dinero like what he did was right. You know what though, Omni? I expected that out of LeeLee and Nek. But out of you? You of all people?! I just knew you would be backing me. I just knew you would be supportive, but you weren't. You straight dogged me because my brother was cheating on you and I didn't tell you. What the fuck? You yell loyalty, but where was the loyalty when I needed you?"

Before I knew it, I had tears pouring from my eyes. Like, I've been so strong during this entire thing... dealing with the fact that my girls just didn't understand what I was going through and stuff... that now, I was just letting it all out. I couldn't believe Omni had turned her back on me after all I've gone through.

True enough, my brothers and Cassim had taken care of him, but that didn't heal the wounds. Omni knew firsthand that I was just damn good at being strong about certain things, but sometimes I needed people. Sometimes I needed my girl, and at that time I needed her. I didn't need the ridicule she gave me behind cheating on Dinero. I didn't need the ridicule she gave me because I chose to have an abortion. Even if she couldn't understand or relate, all she had to do was be there.

She stood up and walked over to me with her arms out, "Oh Ryann." She hugged me and pressed her face against mine, "I love you boo. I'm so sorry that I wasn't there. I'm so sorry that I let the stress of my own problems spill over into our friendship.

*

After Omni and I 'kissed and made up' she helped me pack and I filled her in on everything that was going on in my life and relationship. She was happy for me. And not that fake happy... I could see that she was truly, genuinely happy that I was happy. What she wasn't happy about was the friendship I'd formed with Sinn. She said she felt like Sinn was taking her place. Omni's ass was irreplaceable, even with the shady shit she pulled by turning her back on me.

She and Juice were still going through things. She didn't trust him anymore, but she loved him and because of that, she stayed. Stupid. Stupid as fuck if you ask me but hell, who am I to judge right? I just had an abortion and was cheating on my boyfriend. If Omni wants to play Juice's fool then so be it. I won't say shit else about it.

Now, I was back at Cassim's—oops wait... back home with Cassim, about to get more of my things settled in. I'd already had a key so, when I made it to the door, I just walked right in.

I greeted him with a smile, "Hey babe—

"Ryann... Did you have an abortion," he suddenly asked, causing me to fucking shudder.

What? Who told him? How did he find out?

"What—what are you talking about," I asked with a nervous giggle.

He pinched the bridge of his nose with a menacing laugh, "Yooo, just answer the fuckin' question, darlin'."

I frowned and drew back, "*Darlin*? Where is all of this coming from?"

I dropped my duffle bag on the floor and it crashed against it with a loud, echoic thud. The house was quiet, with the exception of birds that sang right outside of the door. They were happy. So, full of life. Life I wasn't sure I'd be full of if I told him yes.

I was caught between a rock and a hard place. On one hand, I needed to be honest, but on the other hand, I needed to lie. I didn't want this conversation to ever come up. How is it that, nearly three months later, it comes up? How did he find out? There was nothing I could do at this point.

Cassim stood up and slowly approached me with his fist balled and tight lips, "Answer. The. Fucking. Question Ryann. Did you or did you not kill my child?"

How was I supposed to answer that question? I didn't know who's baby it was so I got rid of it. Why was he even asking me that question? How did he even know? Did Omni tell him? Nah... I know my girl ain't shady like that. Like... why would she do this? No one knew besides her. So who else?

"Ryann," he yelled in a booming voice.

I flinched with tears in my eyes. What was happening? Everything was just perfect. Everything between us had been going wonderful. I was the happiest I'd ever been. Now... Now it felt like everything was crashing and burning.

"I don't know," I said as my heart raced.

He looked down at me with cold, black eyes. There was no trace of love. Nothing but pain and anger. Where was that twinkle of love I'd usually see when he was upset with me? Had the love really gone away? That fast?

"Yes or no question, Ryann," he asked through clenched teeth.

"I can't—

His nostrils flared and he gave me another sinister laugh, "Did you or did you not have an abortion?"

"Yes, I had one."

Before I could finish my statement, he walked away with a handful of his dreads. He paced the middle of the living room, in circles, with his dreads in his fist, and his head up to the ceiling. I didn't know what to do. I couldn't move. I had never seen him like this before. His behavior kind of reminded me of Gooses' behavior. Especially when he began to crack up and talk about me like I wasn't standin there.

"Fraud ass bitch," he mumbled. "Fraud ass bitch— yo, get the fuck up out of my crib before I wreck you."

I approached him with my hands out, "Cassim.. listen—

"Call me Cass like the rest of the ho's do," he spat with his top lip curled up. "I asked for honesty... some real shit..." he paused, "That's my bad though, for putting my trust in anybody. I thought shorty was real though. I thought she was special. Bitch is just a fraud. Like the rest of 'eem."

"Aight, listen, I won't be too many more bitches and ho's nigga. I know you're mad but—

He stopped pacing and made a mad dash for me. I flinched, and ran backwards, in fear for my life. As I ran backwards, I tripped over my duffle bag. I was defeated as he stared down at me like a raging bull with his dreads now messily all over his head, and his mouth turned down in a disgusted frown.

"You killed my kid," he yelled, close to my face, spitting in my face.

Cassim grabbed my jaw, and held onto it with so much force that I thought it would crumble into dust, "I should kill you, you...you evil fuckin—

"I... I didn't know if it was yours or his," I said before he could do anything else to me. Before the word bitch could slip off his lips again.

I expected his eyes to soften, but they didn't. I expected the grip on my chin to weaken, but it didn't. He stared at me with the same scowl and gripped my jaw with the same force. He threw my head back and it crashed against the duffle bag.

I sat up straight, and watched Cassim walk away with his shoulders slumped over.

"I'm sorry," I yelled.

He said nothing.

"I'm sorry, Cassim. I'm so sorry."

"Get out. Leave my key on the coffee table." He looked over his shoulder at me, "The rest of your shit will be delivered to you."

I jumped up and ran after him, "So this is it!? Nigga you're breaking up with me?! Because I didn't want to—

He stopped walking, and I ran into his broad back, "If you want to live, it's in your best interest to leave."

I wrapped my arms around his back, and lied my head on it, "Please, Cassim. Think about it from m—

He roughly snatched my arms from around his body and walked off, "Nothing to think about. Get the fuck out. Last warning."

There was a coldness in his tone of voice that petrified me. But I couldn't leave. I didn't move a muscle. I stood there in a daze. Was this really happening? Was he really leaving me? I didn't... I didn't deserve this. I know I messed up by getting the abortion behind his back. Maybe things would have gone differently had I told him? I didn't tell him because if he knew I was pregnant, he would have wanted me to keep it. I couldn't. not with the risks in line. Why couldn't Cassim just understand that?

"I'm not—I'm not leaving," I said as tears poured from my eyes.

*

After sitting in the middle of the living room for thirty minutes, there was a knock on the front door. When Cassim finally came downstairs, I stood up and smiled, hoping that he would say something to me. Hoping that, that look on his face would be gone. But it wasn't. He still wore that deadly scowl. He didn't even look at me. He walked right by me, like I wasn't standing there.

I turned around, watching him answer the door. When he did, I sucked my teeth.

My brothers were here. All three of them slapped hands with Cassim like he wasn't the bad guy in this situation.

He stood at the door with his arms crossed over his chest, "I told her to leave. She wouldn't. I didn't want to hurt her... so yeah, get her up outta my spot."

Juice nodded, and he mobbed over to me. I hated for them to see me like this. I was distraught with dried tears and snot all over my face. I stood there, rapidly shaking my head from side to side.

"Cassssim... no.. don't do this. Do you know? Do you fucking know what this is going to do to me?" I yelled at the top of my lungs as Goose effortlessly picked me up and tossed me over his shoulder.

Cassim didn't care. He didn't give a shit about the tantrum I was throwing. He didn't care about the pain dripping from my voice with every fucking word I spoke. He was unmoved by it. I wanted Goose to let me down. I wanted Cassim to look in my eyes one last time. I wanted him to see how fucking destroyed I was going to be without him... without us.

I beat on Goose's head and back, not giving a fuck about how crazy he was. I wanted to be put down. I didn't want to go back to that house. I wanted to... I wanted to stay with Cassim. I wanted to lie in his arms tonight, and to wake up in them in the morning. What would life become without him? Got damnit! He had just gotten out of jail. I went crazy during those two days without him... and now... now you're telling me I have to spend the rest of my life without him?

How?

Chapter Thirteen . Cass

Shit had been crazy for me over the past few days. Ever since I found out Ryann had an abortion, nothing had been right in my world. It didn't matter that the baby she was carrying could have been the Uber driver's. It didn't matter that she was scared. What fuckin' mattered was the fact that it could have very well been mine. What fuckin' mattered was she lied to me. And with a clear conscious.

After I was told about the abortion, I sat in the crib, on the couch, waiting for her to come back. I didn't even get up and shoot the moves I had to make. I couldn't. I was a raging bull. I was in no mood for business. If I would have left that house in the mood I was in, I would have caught a couple of bodies. If anybody would have looked at me wrong, or played with me on that goofy joking shit, I would have broken a niggas neck. I was just that heated.

I sat there, thinking about all of the times she had a chance to tell me what was what. That morning, I posted up at her hotel room waiting for her to walk in was probably when she was getting the procedure done. She never answered my question of her whereabouts. And I let her. Because then, I was more worried about her wellbeing than I was about where she'd been all morning.

Ryann had plenty of chances to tell me about the abortion after that. So many nights, I laid up with shorty doing absolutely nothing but kicking it. She could have told me then. Perhaps, maybe then I wouldn't have reacted the way I did.

So, like I said, I sat there waiting for Ryann to come home. I waited for her to walk through those doors with that smile on her face like she hadn't just had my baby vacuumed up outta her.

She reacted the way I expected her to react. She tried to dance around the question, but I wasn't for all of that bullshit. As soon as she said yeah, I was finished with her. The tears pouring down her face... shit did nothing to me. I shut her out of my life. For months, I put Ryann on a pedestal. Told her how perfect she was—shit, told you how perfect she was. I thought finding her was like finding a ruby in a pile full of foggy ass rhinestones. Come to find out, she was just like the rest.

I burped and tossed the empty Hennessey bottle into the trashcan across from me. Well, I tried to. I missed it by an inch or two and it went crashing against the pavement.

"You are a complete mess," said Symphony after getting up from her lounger.

She whisked past me and grabbed the push broom that was leaning against the brick behind me, "I sure hope that's your last bottle for the day."

I was on my third pint of Hennessey, with no intentions to let up. I wanted to front and say that the whole situation with Ryann wasn't eating at me. But it'd be a lie. It was eating at me, horribly. I wasn't upset with my decision to leave her. I was upset with her decision to force me to. She knew off top how I felt about kids. Didn't give a fuck though. Shorty wasted no time to open her legs and let them rip a part of me from her body. Straight up said fuck me and my feelings. She knew that I would have been against it. She knew that the chances of it being bitch boys wouldn't have bothered me. So she took it upon herself to make a decision that wasn't hers to make alone.

I thought I would never be able to call Ryann selfish. But she was. It was like, Mask off with shorty. For months, she's been wearing masks. I felt like a sucka. I let up and let my guard down. Fucked around and fell in love, something I should have never done. I should have just fucked her and left her the way I do all of the women that enter my life. The fuck was I thinking? I didn't even trust myself. But I put trust in her.

"Where are your car keys, Cassim," asked Symphony.

I was at Luck's crib, wishing this bitch wasn't here. She had been popping up more often, being nice and shit, but I wanted absolutely no conversation from her. She had alternative motives, and I wanted her far the fuck away from me.

"Man, what," I asked as I pulled the brim of my fitted cap down over my eyes. "Fuck you asking for? Shouldn't you be at home, playing Susie Homemaker or some shit, shorty?"

She laughed and sat down in the lounger next to me. She playfully hit my knee and said, "When have you ever known me as a Susie Homemaker?" She paused, "Shouldn't you be at home with what's-her-face?"

"Stop fronting like you don't remember her name," I shot back with a smirk.

"Neither of them are of importance, now, are they," she sultrily asked like I still found her sexy.

"You really trying to fuck me, with that engagement ring on yo finger? Still a shiesty ass bitch, I see," I said before pushing myself up from the lounger.

She pushed me back down and straddled me. Drunk and all that, I was still able to push her off of me. I wasn't into Symphony like that anymore. Bitch is a truly missing a few marbles. She's not a bad lookin' broad.

She's actually pretty as hell, with a sick ass body, but the bitch can't get my dick hard.

I grabbed her arms and tossed her over onto the lounger next to me. Standing up, I fished around my pockets for my car keys. As soon as I grabbed them out, she snatched them from me.

"You want them back? Come get them," she said before switching off.

I scratched the top of my head with a frown on my face. My phone started to ring. I grabbed it from my pocket, as I followed behind Symphony. Looking at the screen, I sucked my teeth and stuffed it back into my pocket. I could have added her to the block list. I should have. But for some reason, I hadn't.

Ryann had been calling me like crazy. I could only imagine what she was going through right now. Shorty straight lost it when I told her to get out of my crib. She went ape shit. I've never seen Ryann like that before.

"Yo, give me my fuckin' keys, Symphony," I said, as I walked through the sliding doors.

She looked over her shoulder at me, and walked down the basement stairs, "Come get them."

It was after four in the morning. Sinn and Luck were sleep, and this bitch wanted to play games. All I wanted to do was hit the crib and pass out.

I staggered down the stairs, and she giggled, "Be careful, Cassim."

Why the fuck was she even here? I hated that I ever stuck dick to this bitch. She wanted to play games with a nigga who was never really bout 'em. She was only trying this cute shit with me because I was pissy drunk. Otherwise, she wouldn't have even been able to pull this shit on me. Not in my sober state of mine. Not with the obvious look of disgust on my face. But I was drunk, and she was trying to use that to her advantage.

When I made it down the stairs, Symphony was laid out on the couch, ass naked, with her eyes wide open, "Fuck my keys at, Symphony?"

She sat them onto of her bare pussy mound, "Right here."

She bit her lip and played with her nipples as I made my way to the couch. I reached down, and grabbed my keys, but she grabbed my wrist before I could snatch them up.

"Look at me Cassim. Look at my pussy. Remember the way she use to squirt for you?"

I tried to snatch my arm away, but I staggered a little, and got dizzy. Those three pints of Hennessey was doing me dirty at this point.

"Yoooo, what the fuck are you doin' shorty," I asked as she placed my hand on her wet pussy and began to grind on it.

"I know you miss it, Cass. I miss it," she said before reaching out to grab my soft dick with her freehand.

I didn't miss it. I stopped missing it when I had to stop myself from killing her stupid ass. When I say Symphony is a real ass psychotic type broad, I mean it. She came at me with a knife, and I knocked her ass out. It took Luck and Sinn to pull me off that dumb, bird ass bitch. Our 'situationship' was toxic.

"Watch out, Symphony," I said with a laugh. "You wylin', my baby."

She pried my hand open and snatched the keys out of it. Then she took my finger, and dipped it inside of her pussy. She moaned and began to beg for the dick.

"Can't fuck with a soft dick, darlin," I said, steady laughing. "That shit is dead baby. I'm smooth on the twat."

I was drunk as fuck at this point. I could barely stand up, and was staggering all over the place. If it wasn't for her holding to my wrist, I probably would have fallen a long time ago.

"I can get it hard."

"Wanna bet on it," I asked, with a laugh. I threw my head back, "I'm smooooth on the twat shorty."

She sucked her teeth and let my wrist go. I fell back onto another sofa. I snatched my cap off and tossed it across the room, "Stop fuckin' with me. You a real ass weirdo, Symphony. You like that sick shit. You want a nigga to disrespect that pussy, uh?"

She crawled off the couch, and over to the one I was sitting on. She grabbed my belt buckle and unbuckled it.

I closed my eyes and saw her face.

Not Symphony's. But Ryann's. I tried to push Symphony off me again, but it was pointless. She had my soft dick in her hands, rubbing it all over her face, lips, and tongue.

My eyes shot open, when that mafucka came alive.

"Told you I could get him hard," she gloated.

Chapter Fourteen . Ryann

I couldn't sleep.

It had been three days since I slept.

Three days since we broke up.

Three days since my soul was ripped away from my body.

For three days, I lied here in my own filth looking at the ceiling.

My eyes were dry, swollen, and red from lack of sleep, and excessive crying. I had never been so depressed in my life.

A lot of women might call me weak... A lot of women might say that I'm overreacting. That is because a lot of women haven't experienced the type of love I've experienced with Cassim.

I thought that by now, he would have come to apologize. I just knew that by now, I would be in his arms. But I haven't heard from him. Three days. I've called him. I've texted him, but I've gotten nothing. I thought that maybe he would have dropped by to bring me the rest of my things. But he hadn't. He sent my things back. He sent them back by movers. My boxes cluttered the living room. As I said, I haven't moved a muscle.

Omni had been here. But I didn't have any words for her. I felt like she had betrayed our friendship. I wanted to lash out. I wanted to jump up and confront her. But I couldn't. The only thing I've been able to do was call Cassim. The only thing I've been able to do was think about him. He consumed my every thought. I missed him.

I would go into detail about how much but you know. You know what missing him does to me. My heart didn't beat the same without him. I wasn't the same without him. I was a shell of what I was when I was with him.

I know. I shouldn't give a man so much power over me. And I didn't. It was his love that I gave power. It was his touch. It was his fucking soul. The way...the way it meshed with mine.

Bang... Bang... Bang.

For three nights, all I've heard was a headboard knocking against my wall. The wall I shared with Ashlee. For three nights, I've heard her moaning. For three nights, I've heard his groaning. For three nights, I've heard this shit. I was reaching my breaking point. If it was anything that was going to get me out of my bed was the annoying sound of Ashlee steady fucking Loc in my house.

Like, that nigga got his own shit. Why not go there? Why rub their passion in my face? I didn't care that what they were doing was just fucking. There was still balls slapping against flesh. Dicks getting sucked. Orgasms erupting. All of which I was not getting. I was annoyed. Hearing them only made this worst. Hearing them only made me think of Cassim. Of the way he pampered my pussy with his massive dick. Made me think of the way he feasted on my pussy like my sweet nectar was the sweetest thing he'd ever drank. Hearing them made me think of the way his curved, veiny, thick, delicious dick felt sliding down my throat.

Hearing them reminded me of what I could no longer have.

I snatched the cover off of me so roughly that the tail of it bumped against the plate of uneaten food sitting on my nightstand. Uneaten food prepared by Omni, cluttered with more uneaten food prepared by Goose, Adrien, Nek, Ashlee, and even Juice.

I sat on side of the bed, trying to get myself together before I went stomping out of my room. I grabbed the room temperature bottle water from the floor and twisted the cap off. It was one of many. Water was the only thing I've had in three days. I chugged the whole thing, and tossed the bottle in a nearby trashcan.

I stood up and felt a little lightheaded. Most likely it came from not eating. I needed to get my shit together. I can't go on like this. Again, I've fallen behind on my photography gigs and everything.

I walked out of my room, heading to Ashlee's. I sucked my teeth and rolled my eyes at the moaning she was doing. Moaning she did a bad job at trying to muffle.

"Shhh, wait... wait.. slow down before you wake her up," whispered Ashlee.

Too late. I was already awake. I haven't been asleep. All I asked Ashlee for was a little bit of respect. If she wanted to fuck all up and through the crib, she should just get her own shit. period. Shaneka respects that rule, but her thot ass sister couldn't.

I boldly twisted the doorknob and barged inside. I heard them gasp. In the darkness, I saw them jump. I flicked the light switch on, and nearly passed out at the sight before me. What the fuck type of unholy, nasty, sick, twisted shit is this!?

"Juice?! Juice!? You two.... Are fucking? What the fuck!? We're cousins," I screamed with shaky hands.

Ashlee pulled the thin sheet up over her breast, lowered her head in shame and shook it from side to side.

"Incest?! You bitches are foul! Sick! And fucking foul!!!!!!!!!!!"

All of this time, I thought Ashlee had been fucking Loc up in here. Was it my fucking brother she referred to as 'fucking like a maniac' that day? I felt sick to my stomach, as I turned to go back to my room. I held onto the door frame, as I started to feel faint.

"Please don't mention what you just witnessed," said Juice.

I looked over my shoulder at him with a nasty, hateful glare, "You think I want people to know how fucking foul you are, bitch? You nasty, sick, twisted, crazy bitches!"

*

After seeing what I saw last night, I forced myself to go to sleep. I couldn't stay up. It would be the only thing I thought about. I needed to shut my mind off. I needed to rejuvenate myself too. I slept long and hard. When I did finally wake up, I had three missed calls from Sinn. I couldn't understand why she was hitting me up when I'm quite sure she knows that Cassim... that Cassim and I were taking a break.

That's what I'll call it. Taking a break. All I needed was five minutes with him. All I needed was to grab a hold of his hand. All he needed was to hear my sincerest apology. We could move past this right? We had to. For the sake of my sanity, we had to.

I sat up, and rested up against the headboard to call Sinn back.

"Whew! Thank God you still alive. Bitch, I was about to ride out looking for—

"What's up, Sinn," I said, cutting the dramatics short.

"What's up with you and Cass?"

I frowned, "What? Why?"

"Something is off. I already know something is off. That nigga has been buggin out for the last few days. Do you know he forced my man to play Russian Roulette with him last night? He put a gun to my man's head and told him if he didn't play he would pull the trigger. Na, I love Cass but I'd be damned if—"

"Where is he," I asked with wide eyes.

"In my basement passed out," she said with an attitude. "Na, Luck told me that something happened between you two, but he didn't know what."

"Is it okay if I come by?"

She paused, "I don't know, Ryann. Nate is here, and I really don't want any drama going on in front of him."

I shook my head, "I promise there will be no drama."

I prayed like hell that, that was a promise I could keep. I wasn't sure how I'd respond if Cassim shot me down.

*

I parked in Sinn's driveway behind Cassim's car and checked the mirror before getting out. Before I got here, I stopped at Starbucks for two breakfast sandwiches, and a Grande Caramel Macchiato. I didn't want to look like I was dying of starvation, and like I was exhausted. I wanted Cassim to see me at my absolute best. I had to be on my A-game if I wanted to win this nigga back.

So, I got dressed in some skinny jeans which were slit at the knees, that looked painted on. They accentuated my shape perfectly. I wore an off the shoulder, crop top, and some cute strappy sandals. I made sure I beat my face, and I threw on one of my frontal wigs, and had it bone straight.

I flipped the sun visor back up and took a deep breath before getting out of the car. Barbecue smoke was coming from the backyard, so I went back there instead of knocking on the front door. I could see Nate playing in the pool on a floaty. DJ Khaled's I'm The One played at a low volume from speakers that are usually blasting.

Quavo!
I'm the one that hit that same spot
She the one that bring them rain drops
We go back, remember crisscross and hopscotch
You the one that hold me down when the block's hot
I make your dreams come true when you wake up
And your look's just the same without no make-up
Had to pull up on your mama, see what you're made of
Ain't gotta worry 'bout 'em commas 'cause my cake up

"Hey y'all," I said to Sinn and Luck who were standing at the grill with their backs to me.

Luck looked over his shoulder, sent me a quick head nod and hurried into the house. Sinn shook her head and wiped her hands on the front of her apron, "Hey girl. I didn't tell them you were coming. He's probably going to wake that nigga up."

I stepped onto the deck, fumbling with my keychain, "Can I go inside?"

Sinn lightly chewed on her bottom lip and then said, "Yeah go ahead. But listen... Symphony spent the night last night and—

"And what," I snapped with raised eyebrows.

"Nothing happened... I'm just telling you so that you won't be alarmed when you see her. I know how crazy you are about that nigga, and I don't want you clowning in front of my son, aight?"

I walked off and stormed into the house. Symphony sat at the island sipping from a cup of coffee.

When I walked in, she looked over her shoulder at me with a snort and a dry good morning. I didn't say anything in return, I headed straight for the basement.

"He just woke up. He had a long night," said Symphony sitting there with a smirk, with both hands wrapped around the coffee mug she sipped from.

I snorted, as my eyes averted from her to the pot of coffee siting on the coffee maker. I was about five seconds away from grabbing it and tossing what was left of it in her face.

I wondered, for a spit second, if Cassim had fucked this bitch. Sinn said that he was drunk as hell. Anything could have happened. I could take her being engaged in consideration, but she didn't give a damn about Todd. She was almost as stiff as plywood with him. She seemed like one of those bitches that were only in it for the money. And if that was the case, she wouldn't give a fuck about fucking my dude. Yes, my dude. That break up was one sided. I just been giving him some time to come to his senses. I've had enough now though.

Before I could get down the stairs, he was already climbing them, fixing his disheveled ponytailed dreads.

"Good morning," I said to him.

He looked up at me and kept walking up the stairs. Despite the fact that I was standing there. Despite the fact that I was clearly unmoving. He walked up those stairs like he was going to walk straight through my ass if I didn't move. So, I stood my ass right there. He stood at the step right below the top one and said, "Excuse me, darling."

Symphony giggled. The bitch literally giggled. She knew that when Cassim used the word darling, it was not in a form of flattery.

I narrowed my eyes at him, "Don't call me that shit."

He grabbed my arms and moved me aside.

"Yo, Luck. You saw my car keys," he said as he felt around his pockets for keys.

"I have them. You were trying to leave last night," said Symphony hopping down from the Bristol stool.

I stood there baffled like... why is this bitch trying me? Why are these mothafuckas trying me? I told Sinn I would be cool for the sake of Nate, and I will. I will kindly drag this bitch upstairs and beat her ass up there. He won't see it. I promise he won't know.

Symphony handed Cassim the keys, and he said, "Good lookin'."

"You know I got you," she said as she switched back over to her chair.

I chuckled and licked my lips, "Keep trying me... Keep fuckin' trying me."

Cassim paid me no attention as he moved around the kitchen to where the refrigerator sat. He opened it and grabbed some orange juice from it.

I sucked my teeth, and walked over to him, "You really gone stand there like you don't see me?"

He sipped from the personal sized bottle of orange juice then asked, "What's good *killa*?"

That stung. I knew that was a jab at the abortion I had. He had a smirk on his face, and that bitch... that bitch was steady giggling.

I looked over my shoulder at her, "Bitch you better get the fuck up outta here with that cute shit before I jump over that island and beat the life out of you."

"This is my sister's house. I am welcomed—

"Symphony," said Luck, coming up the basement stairs. "Chill yo. You know Nate out back. Go out there. Help Sinn on the grill."

"What," she said like she was offended.

Luck just stood there staring at her. She turned the mug up to her mouth and hopped down from the Bristol chair. As she walked through the sliding doors that led to the deck, she mumbled some things under her breath.

"Cassim... can we talk," I asked, standing there, steady fumbling with the big puff ball on my keychain.

Cassim's eyes met mine and a cool chill ran down my spine. The love... where was it? He moved around me, tossed the empty juice bottle into the trashcan and told Luck to walk with him.

I felt alone. In a world populated by over seventy-five billion people; I felt alone.

He wasn't going to talk to me. He barely acknowledged my presence. He didn't care about me. The love I'd usually see in his eye contact. That look of 'finding it' was no longer there. Cassim didn't care about me anymore. How? How was it so easy for him to shut feelings out for me? Because I had an abortion? I mean, come on now anybody with sense would have aborted that child.

I stood there in the kitchen unsure of what to do with myself. I had never felt so helpless in my life. I had never felt so lost either. Falling in love with that nigga had been a gift and a curse.

Sinn walked into the kitchen, and I got myself together. I scratched my head and thanked her for calling me about Cassim, but not to do it again.

On my way out of the house, he called my name. My heart skipped a beat, and butterflies filled the pit of my stomach. I quickly turned around with a smile, "Yeah?"

"Tell that nigga Juice to answer his fuckin' phone," he spat with a scowl on his face.

Shattered. My heart, it shattered into a billion pieces. I just nodded and walked out of the house.

When I made the decision to have the abortion, I never factored in how Cassim would feel if he found out. I kind of just brushed it under the rug, thinking that he never would. He found out, and I told him why it happened thinking that, that would change his perspective about things. But it hadn't. And most likely it wouldn't.

"Ryann," said Sinn, jogging up behind me just as I had hit the unlock button on my keychain.

I looked over my shoulder at her, "Yeah?"

"Hold up," she leaned against my car, breathing heavy, tired as hell. "Good lawd, I'd like to faint. Anyway girl," she fanned herself. "Pretend you don't care. You show him that you care too much. Go find you a new nigga, I bet bread he gets his mind right. His mind ain't ever been right. But when he was with you.. he was different. Still... all you gotta do is crawl up under some new dick I bet—"

"I'm straight," I said cutting her off. "I'll be good."

It was a lie. And she knew it was a lie. She'd witnessed me at one of the most vulnerable stages in my life. I almost lost every bit of sanity I had even he was locked up for the short period of time. She knew just like everyone else in my life knew, that this break up—yeah, I can call it that now—was really taking a toll on me.

She placed her hand on my shoulder, "I ain't gotta worry about you pulling a Hannah Baker on me now do I?"

I chuckled and shook my head, "No, girl, I'm not good now, but I will be."

I glanced up at the house, at the sound of the door opening and Cassim was coming out with Luck in tow. He looked over at me, and then quickly looked away. Luck did the same thing. I noticed a glimmer of pity in his gaze though. I hated this. I hated that everybody knew about this breakup. I especially hated that Symphony knew. She had been standing by the gate watching Sinn and I talk the whole time. Straight goofy bitch that had been saved by the promise I made to Sinn about not beating her ass in front of Nate.

"Please call me if you need to talk. Listen, I know we met through that crazy nigga but our friendship don't have to end because y'all relationship did," She waved me off. "He'll be back though. Just let him cool off. His ass is too into you to leave you alone. Trust me. I've been friends with Cass long enough to know that he wife's none! He did that with you. That means you're special."

I smiled a little, "Or, I was special." I sighed and said, "Alright Sinn. Take care."

"Me? Bitch.. you take care. You too fine—

"Bye Sinn," I said with a laugh as I got into the car.

I stared up at him through the tints of my windows. He wore his dark tinted Buffs, but I knew that he was staring back at me too. I could feel it. Like I said before, his eye contact was so strong, that it was like he had lasers shooting from his pupils. And although, I couldn't see those black pearls called irises, I knew he was looking at me.

*

I couldn't just give up.

I needed him alone. So, I followed behind him. I kept my distance so that he wouldn't know I was creeping though. In the direction we were going, I knew that we were heading to the house. I didn't need to be on his tail to get to that place.

I know. I must look pretty fuckin' pitiful right now but this love I share with Cassim... it's not one to just give up on. I'm fighting for this shit. And I'm going to force him to talk to me. I'm going to force him to touch me. If I could get him to do that, I'd win off rip.

As I was riding behind him, two police cars sped in front of me and hit their sirens, pulling him over. My heart rate sped up, and I pressed my foot down on the gas pedal. What the fuck was going on, now? Why were they always bothering him? Cassim wasn't speeding. He was driving, minding his own business. What the hell was this about? I swallowed as I gripped the steering wheel, slowing up at the scene.

He'd stopped, and five cops approached his car with their guns drawn. I stopped and snatched my seatbelt off. I got out of the car, getting ready to approach him. We were just getting ready to get on the freeway and were driving on the service drive. There were cars riding behind me, but I didn't care. I didn't care about walking the streets of a busy road. I didn't like how they were pulling him over. With guns out, aggressively telling him to step out of the vehicle and shit, like he was a criminal.

I mean, duh, he is a criminal, but he had done absolutely nothing wrong.

"Hands on the back of your head," yelled one of the cops when Cassim finally got out of the car.

He saw me.

Our eyes locked before he was forced against the car.

"What is this about—

"You're under arrest for the murder of James, Sandra, and Shondra McGee...."

Everything after that was like a blur. This was not like before—when he was wanted down at the station for questioning. Oh no... they said he was under arrest... for the murder. A murder I knew he didn't commit. Why were they placing him under arrest for this? What happened?

I slammed my car door, and ran towards them, "What—No! Let him go! He didn't do anything. He—he didn't kill them! Cassim—

Crash!

Before I knew it, the wind had been knocked out of me and I was thrown up into the air. I didn't realize what had happened until I went crashing down onto the roof of a car I never saw coming.

-TBC-

Facebook @ : Author Miss'Candice
Instagram @ : misscandice.theauthor

CPSIA information can be obtained
at www.ICGtesting.com
Printed in the USA
LVHW050112180519
618323LV00001B/61/P